ONCE UPON AN ELEPHANT

ONCE UPON AN ELEPHANT

*a down to earth tale of Ganesh
and what happens when worlds collide*

ASHOK MATHUR

ARSENAL PULP PRESS
Vancouver

ARSENAL PULP PRESS
103-1014 Homer Street
Vancouver, B.C.
Canada V6B 2W9
www.arsenalpulp.com

The publisher gratefully acknowledges the support of the Canada Council of the Arts for its publishing program, as well as the support of the Book Publishing Industry Development Program, and the B.C. Arts Council.

Printed and bound in Canada by Printcrafters

Portions of this novel have appeared in *West Coast Line*, *Prairie Fire*, and *Contours of the Heart: South Asians Map North America* (Asian American Writers' Workshop).

CANADIAN CATALOGUING IN PUBLICATION DATA:
Mathur, Ashok.

Once upon an elephant

ISBN 1-55152-058-3

I. Title.
PS8576.A8286052 1998   C813'.54   C98-910433 8
PR9199.3.M397052 1998

ACKNOWLEDGEMENTS

thanks

to Ganesha (who actually wrote most of this);

to my parents, Perin and Parshottam;

to friends and colleagues who have played some part in this project, either directly or in some obscure way: Hiromi Goto, Larissa Lai, Aruna Srivastava, Sharron Proulx, Tamai Kobayashi, Fred Wah, Sonia Smee, Roy Miki, Jeff Derksen, Mark Nakada, Louise Saldanha, Jennifer Kelly, Aritha van Herk, Rita Wong, Linda Chen, Hank Bull, Nicole Markotic, Rajinderpal S. Pal, Tony Snow, Asha Varadharajan, Suzette Mayr and, as always, Minquon Panchayat;

to sources cited or alluded to:

Rushdie, Salman. *Midnight's Children*. Jonathon Cape. London. 1981.

Shastir, J. L. ed. *Siva Purana*. Motilal Banarsidass Publishers. 1978.

Spivak, Gayatri Chakravorty. "Can the Subaltern Speak?" in *Marxism and the Interpretation of Culture*. Eds. Cary Nelson and Lawrence Grossberg. Urbana and Chicago: University of Illinois Press, 1998: 271-313.

Varadharajan, Asha. *Exotic Parodies: Subjectivity in Adorno, Said, and Spivak*. Minneapolis and London: University of Minnesota, 1995.

Worswick, Clark and Embree, Ainslie, eds. *The Last Empire: Photography in British India, 1855-1911*. Millerton NY: An Aperture Book, 1976.

to The Writers' Guild of Alberta and The Canada Council for financial assistance provided for this project;

and to The Leighton Studios at the Banff Centre, most particularly to Douglas Cardinal's wonderful studio with its windows opening out onto a world of elk, coyote, and mountains.

PRELUDE

Was it I who wrote that consumed multitudes are jostling and shoving inside me? It could have been me who wrote that, but it wasn't, or maybe it was and I don't remember. I also might have written, in the same place (unless it wasn't me), that I have been the swallower of lives and to know me, just the one of me, you'll have to swallow the lot as well. No, the mystery here is that those are not my words, just as *these* are not my words, unless they are and they aren't. The multitudes inside? Let's start with the easiest, the most recognizable, the statuesque, potbellied, elephant-headed Ganesh. He's inside me everywhere, but if I am truly to believe that I'm such a life-swallower, he must be everywhere outside me too. So his name evokes all those other Ganeshes, the sandalwood Ganeshes and stone Ganeshes and silk Ganeshes, living all around me and, if this story is true, whoever tells it, around and inside you, too. He can think. He can reason. He can swallow. Always back to that. Who else is inside? Ganapati, of course, the wise one, no different in appearance, or so they say, except as leader of his father's famous troops, his ganas, Ganapati is indeed wiser and more robust than one might imagine. And let me not forget the hereafter invisible Vighnesvara, elephant-headed of course, but an investigator in his own right, lord and destroyer of obstacles and competent interrogator of canine and ungulate alike. Oh, but there are more, many more, and in the distance I hear that stolen voice again saying there are those who will trample me underfoot, reduce me to specks of voiceless dust, a veritable legion of elephant-headed princes whose names evoke passion and success (that's where Siddhi comes in, sometimes known as a consort, sometimes as yet another avatar of Lord Ganesh, sometimes as something in-between, as that magical or spiritual power for the control of self, others, and the forces of nature). See, nobody said swallowing the world would be easy. Just be glad that I have no stomach for all the others, for the one-tusked one known as Eka Danta, for the one with a bent trunk known as Vakratunda, for the one particularly noted for his elephant ears, Gaja Karnaka, or for the one hundred and eight, the one thousand and eight manifestations and variations of this annihilating whirlpool of multitudes. But inside me, deep inside, digesting slowly away is a judiciary, a legal establishment and its concomitant constabulary, all mingling excitedly with Ganeshes, Siddhis, Ganapatis, Vighnesvaras, truly a colossal collision of tastes and sensations. Consumed, consumable multitudes, rushing to tell their stories.

JUDGE McECHERN

"All rise."

Everyone rises.

Judge McEchern walks in, robed in black, sighs as he negotiates the three steps up to his judge table, sets himself down, squints out at the courtroom. Another dreary day, he thinks. Stupid caseload. He squints harder at the courtroom, tries to identify any troublemakers he might be able to cite for contempt. He likes citing spectators for contempt. He's proud that he's cited more spectators for contempt than any other judge on the Queen's Bench. He doesn't put up with any guff from spectators. No fooling around in his courtroom. He squints. Tawdry looking bunch. A few foreigners. He doesn't say things like this aloud any more because of those pesky young lawyers who keep sniffing around, looking for any excuse to prove he's gone off the deep end, senile maybe, or at least some sort of monstrous xenophobe. That's what the editorial columnist for the *Star* called him. Xenophobe. Just because he speaks his mind, doesn't put up with any guff from anyone, whether they're coloured or normal. No guff. He squints.

He squints even harder just in case he's mistaken.

He looks around cautiously to see if anyone else has noticed. His mind is as sharp as ever, but he has to admit his eyesight is getting a bit dim. But, no, he's sure, even if no one else has noticed.

"Ahem."

The Crown Prosecutor looks up at him nervously. The legal aid lawyer looks up at him nervously. The clerk looks up at him nervously.

"Ahem. Could someone please tell me if this is a courtroom or a Hallowe'en party?"

Eyes shuffle nervously. The question is rhetorical, but everyone knows the pattern of the court. Judge McEchern will repeat the question until someone tries to answer, then he'll interrupt and answer his own question. That's how it always goes.

"Hello? Will someone *please* tell me if this is a courtroom or a Hallowe'en party?"

A count of three and the Crown rises. She adjusts her collar. She begins to speak.

"If it please the court —"

"It would *certainly* please the court," Judge McEchern interrupts, "if members of the gallery treated this court with a minute amount of respect and did *not* appear dressed up like damned football mascots."

He pauses for effect. He likes to pause for effect. Gives people some time to stew. Then he can hit 'em with contempt if they speak out of turn. He was up to thirty-six contempt charges this year but it was already November. In 1986 he had charged forty-nine insolent bastards with contempt and he was determined to break that record this year.

"I think we all know whom I'm addressing." He squints even harder now so that his eyes close completely and he has to open them a titch so he can see people's reactions. He hopes no one notices his eyes were completely closed because then people would start to talk like they did about Judge Hargood who actually used to wake himself up by snoring too loud in the courtroom, at least before they put him on medication. Judge McEchern wonders how ol' Harry Hargood is doing and makes a mental note to look him up, although he always promptly forgets any mental notes he makes, which is why he has to write things down these days.

The Crown speaks again, still tugging at her collar.

"Your Worship, if it please the court, I believe there exists a minor misunderstanding, perfectly explicable of course, and which has the effect of creating some confusion; however, if it please the court —"

"*Miz* Block," interrupts Judge McEchern, intentionally elongating and accentuating the honorific so it sounds simultaneously redundant and offensive, "it *would* please the court if you would explain why a member of the gallery is dressed up like a bloody jungle animal!"

"He's not dressed up," the Crown retorts, almost petulantly. "That's the way he is."

"That — that thing, that head? You're telling me that this — this *person* in my courtroom has an elephant head?"

The Crown smiles and nods.

Judge McEchern is silent. He is confused. There is an elephant in his courtroom, a gallery full of foreigners, a woman Crown prosecutor, and he hasn't the slightest idea what to do.

"Court will recess for lunch," he says, fully aware of the multiple sets of eyes which glance clockward and note that it is ten minutes past ten in the morning. For emphasis, Judge McEchern decides to rap his gavel like they do on TV. He reaches out for his gavel and grasps for it. It is not until his hand begins to close that he notices the clerk has failed to put his gavel in its place. Then Judge McEchern remembers that Court of Queen's Bench judges don't actually have gavels. That's only on American TV. Judge McEchern feels foolish.

He opens his hand and bangs on his bench two times, hard, with his palm.

He thinks he must look like those goofy MPs when they're making noises of approval on that House of Commons cable channel.

Judge McEchern is very glad they don't let television cameras into Canadian courtrooms.

SIMPSON

Delilah's my partner. Not like in real life, just work. In real life, no, that'd be different. 'Course, the guys at the detachment are always giving me a hard time, mainly cuz D's the only woman on our watch. They don't give her enough credit, really. She knows her stuff. I gotta admit that when we first got assigned together, I had a bit of that suspicion, too. Up 'til then the watch had been all guys. Most of the force, actually, was all guys. Sometimes I joke about that being the reason I joined. But I only share the joke with D. The boys, well, they wouldn't understand. So me and D work together, have for almost two years now, and we've had our share of strange cases – but this one, well. . . . When the call came through on the radio, neither of us really believed it. Sounded too far-out, even for Alberta. But when we got there, sure enough. It was down in the river valley, and there were already four of our guys down there looking real confused. D saw the bodies first. Or I should say body, singular. Or I dunno. Anyway, D's outta the car like a shot and I stop to talk to the guys for a second, and before I know it D's back and she's just shaking her head like she couldn't make head or tail out of this. Head or tail. That's kinda a joke, too, I guess. So I go take a look. He was down the embankment in a pile of oxtails. I guess I shouldn't say "he" cuz all that was there was this head, very neatly severed at the neck. One good clean blow, no doubt. A guillotine couldn't have done better. Anyway, "he" was all of eighteen, maybe, and, I tell ya right now, gorgeous. A real prince, that one. South Asian in him for sure, but he coulda been mixed cuz the skin was quite light, almost bronze. And if I hadn't seen the neat red line where his neck suddenly stopped from turning into his body, I'd have said he was sleeping as peaceful as a baby. But, there was that missing torso that certainly confused things. Of course, there was a torso next to the head, but it clearly wasn't his. I wanted to cradle that beautiful head, tell him it'd all be all right, but that seemed downright silly, so I just looked over at D and she looked at me, and we both shrugged.

PARVATI

Men never listen. Or when they listen they don't get it. So you tell one man you want a child and he laughs at you, goes off dancing with god knows how many bimbos, figuring you can want all you want but without him there will be no baby. Like you need him for *that*. So you tell another man, look boy, you want to have a bath in privacy so just stand outside and don't let anyone in, a simple request you would think, and he goes and loses his head over it. And then you confront the wouldbe/wannabe father of your child that it's up to him to make reparations, and what does he go and do? Goes on a killing spree, that's what he does, and then has the audacity to say it's your fault. Men never listen. Or when they listen, they fuck up.

DELILAH

I saw the bodies before Simpson did. He was too busy hanging with the guys, doing what I call that bondage thing. Me and Simpson joke about things like that. Anyway, what blew me away wasn't so much the guy's head – maybe not an everyday occurence, but I've seen similar and worse – but the body laying half in, half out of the river. I didn't have to rely on my two years of veterinary science to tell me that what we had here was one massive, headless pachyderm. Now, I've seen cattle with all sorts of body parts missing, mutilations of various kinds, but nothing quite like this. I looked at Simpson and he looked at me and we both shrugged and I knew we were thinking the same thing: okay, so here were the remnants, but where was the guy's body and where was the beast's head?

So Simpson and me shrugged and he looked at me and said, "If and when we find the killer, I'll let you take first crack at him," which made me smile mainly because we both knew that whoever had hacked off this elephant's head must be mighty handy with whatever massive instrument he was using.

Thank god I work with Simpson and not with one of those other turds. I mean, he's still a guy, but he's cool and we do good work together. We're good cops, we tell each other, just like they do on every stupid cop show. I tell him he's Lacey to my Cagney, but I don't push that one too far or he gets pissed at me. The guys, well, they just call us Simpson and Delilah, which makes everyone laugh, especially if someone starts singing – and someone always does – that Springsteen song. Romeo and Juliet, Sampson and

Delilah, all that stuff about great romantic loves. Of course, they wouldn't be thinking that if they knew any better, but we keep things to ourselves like good partners, "good cops," should. One thing I can never figure out is why I always get called Delilah instead of Watson and Simpson's called Simpson instead of Gregor. I guess Gregor and Watson just doesn't mean anything.

PARVATI

In vitro is for sissies. Here's whatcha do:

Take one part clay, one part soil, shake some sweat on it, mix well with water – preferably from a holy river source – let stand, shape into desired form, take a deep breath, blow. Presto.

No morning nausea, no breathing exercises, no delivery decisions.

No breastfeeding, no baby formula, no diaper mess, no diaper rash.

No terrible twos or terrifying threes.

Just instant family.

Cool.

Unless *someone* fucks up.

VIGHNESVARA

I swear I'd forget my head sometimes if it wasn't screwed on ha ha ha. Now now, shouldn't make fun of myself, tusk tusk. Hoo-boy. I'm the one. It's all my fault. I'm the one who makes history. I write it down word by word by word until the story's done. Ain't nuthin gonna stand in mah way. See, it was like this, I was just standing there, just *standing* there, when this dude comes along and tells me to move aside. Move aside, I say, not hardly likely, though if truth be known I wasn't sure what I was standing there for in the first place. But step aside, remove the obstacle, never. So this dude pulls a Little John tactic, 'cept in that story the hardware was a staff and in this story, my story, we're talking sabre. But I'll get back to that later. Do you have any idea how hard it is to interrupt your own story and write it down as you're doing so? Talk about obstacles. *Man.* But let me tell you this. Around the world they're feeding me milk. Cow's milk, goat's milk, mother's milk. One percent, two percent, homogenized, unpasteurized, half and half, soy, rice. Milk milk milk. You name it, they're feeding it to me. Mostly I take it because it's time, but occasionally even I've had my fill. But back to that story later. Right now all you need to know is my Robin Hood was no match for his Little John. I know I shouldn't say this, because that's not how it's written and all, but since I'm doing the writing, I'm going to say it anyway, which is I should have stepped aside. But, no sense crying over spilled milk.

MR. S

So these cops come by and they starts asking me questions. Where were ya, what were ya doin' on the night of, that sorta thing. Then this one cop, the guy, he pulls out a picture, shows me a photograph, see, of my shiv. Now, I gotta tell ya, this shiv of mine's no ordinary blade. Like if I were to tell ya where I got it – nah, never mind. So it's my shiv all right, a big one it is, and really I got nothing to hide, so I sez yeah, it's mine, what of it. That's when the woman, she starts to say I'm not under arrest or nuthin but they wanna ask me a few questions at the station, and that's when I start freakin' out a bit, see, cuz I don't really know where that shiv is anymore and I know by now that the only reason these cops is gonna be asking me about the blade, y'know, is if it somehow got involved in some sort of crime scene. And if it did, and since I already said it was mine, I know sure's shooting that I could be in deep shit. And the only thing I can think of is that it's got somethin' to do with Parvati and that damn kid, that's what I think. Shit.

Grisly remains found

FELIX DOLAN
Police Reporter

A bizarre discovery of human and animal remains in the lower river valley Tuesday has left police investigators stymied.

Police said body parts of a male, between 20 and 30, and an as-yet undetermined animal were reported to police by a couple who were fishing in the area.

The condition of the remains suggest the man was killed recently, said Staff-Sergeant Henry Cooper, although time of death has not been confirmed.

Police are looking for anyone who might have seen anything unusual in the river valley area on Monday or Tuesday.

PARVATI

People love to tell stories of beginnings and endings, births and deaths, marriages and divorces. Most of all, though, people love to tell stories about you, your stories, as if some sort of divine power has sewn your mouth shut so you can barely utter a sound, let alone tell stories, unless the entire story consists of sounds like *mmmm, nnngggg,* and *uuufffff.*

Here are some of the stories they like to tell.

Story #1:

Siva and you, sporting (they actually say "sporting") in the jungle when we chance upon a pair of elephants, similarly engaged in sporting. And they figure the import of that event was so overwhelming that the offspring of our sport is cute little pot-bellied, elephant-headed Ganesh. Sure, why not?

Story #2:

Those nasty bad demons get too powerful and poor old Shiva — they spell his name with an "h" sometimes to *enshure* the reader remembers to shhh instead of ssss — has to do something to keep them in line, so he creates cute, little, pot-bellied, elephant-head Ganesh, lord of obstacles, to put hindrances in their way. Neat little story that one; notice that you're not in it?

Story #3:

You're the jealous type, that's what they say, and being the jealous type it's you, what with your womanly wiles and witchy curses, that turns the princely head of Siva's son, Ganesh, into that of an elephant. Sure, no problem. Fairly common, after all, for women to disfigure their sons so their husbands pay less attention to their boys, right? Happens all the time.

Yes, the above are a bit dumpy and dull, which is why you try to promote the last and, as far as you're concerned, truest account of events.

Story #4:

Siva doesn't feel like hanging around you much these days. And when you broach the idea of, say, starting a family, why not, you both have a reasonable income being deities and all, and lots of time for child-rearing and whatnot, Siva does this fastback moonwalk and says, *Goin' dancin, see ya later.* So you, in a bit of irritation, decide to sweat out your frustration. Maybe you do the video workout thing, maybe it's the dry sauna in the woods, doesn't really matter. Point is, you notice this sweat dripping off your very worshippable body and you figure, again being a goddess and all, to make some use of this, so you shape the sweat into a handsome lad whom you call your son, Ganesh. Then, figuring your body could use a good soak after all this sweating and creating, you decide to take a dip; as an afterthought you think to put your newly-fashioned son to use and ask him to guard your bathing chambers, just in case any of those god-to-god salesmen come traipsing by your holy quarters. So you have your bath, a good relaxing time, and emerge from the tub and your chambers only to find the following scene: said son's body, lying in a heap, his once-attached head a bounce and a roll away in the corner; Siva, shuffling apprehensively from foot to foot, sheepish grin on his face, in his hand that enormous sword, still dripping from blood that came from your sweat. You don't have to ask what happened. You just look at the oaf people call your consort and he begins to babble: wanted to see ya, didn't know he was yours, he shouldn't't've got in the way of a god . . . that sort of thing. Well, well, well, just what is Siva planning to do about this trail of stupidity? And that's when he suggests a plan only a god could love. He will, he announces, take the head from the very first beast who passes by and place it on the shoulders of your (our, he says, winkingly) son, thereby bringing Ganesh-boy back to life. Before you can protest, before you can suggest there lies in the corner a perfectly good head that actually fits quite well on this particular body and you should know because you put it there with your own sweat, off gallops Siva to find himself a jungle beast. And he does, blahblahblah, the story is written and all that.

What remains unwritten, though, is this story here. What to do, you ask Siva, with the headless body of an elephant, the princely head of your son. I'll take care of it, says Siva.

Right, you say.

And you wonder what sort of stories they'll tell about you this time.

JUDGE McECHERN

Judge McEchern is not having a good day. He has just returned from a three-hour lunch during which time he ate nothing because he wasn't hungry. Now that he's back on the bench, his stomach growls to tell him he is hungry, but he knows he can't very well call another lunch break, even though he toys with the idea. He is still perturbed that there is an elephant in his courtroom. Judge McEchern glares at the elephant. The elephant appears oblivious. During the lunch break his court clerk has told him that this is an unusual case. The Crown Prosecutor has told him that this is an unusual case. The legal aid lawyer has told him that this is an unusual case. Judge McEchern wonders why everyone tells him what is patently obvious. What he wants people to tell him is that this is all a mistake, that he doesn't have to be here in his own courtroom trying to stare down an elephant, that he can go home to a snifter of brandy and review tomorrow's very normal-sounding docket. But no one tells him this. Instead, they wait to see what he will do. Judge McEchern sighs.

"Well, *Miz* Block, how would you like to proceed?" asks Judge McEchern. He asks this instead of asking for a plea from the defence because the Crown has suggested this is not going to be a normal case. Like he didn't know.

"I – uh – um, normally I – uh – don't know, Your Honour."

At least she's honest.

Judge McEchern looks over to the defence table. The legal aid lawyer is very young. Judge McEchern has never seen him before. The legal aid lawyer has his black hair slicked back and tied into a two-inch ponytail. Judge McEchern can see this because the legal aid lawyer is suddenly very attentive to an assortment of papers, which apparently are in dire need of immediate shuffling. As he shuffles papers importantly inside an attaché case on his desk, his two-inch ponytail bobs up and down and Judge McEchern thinks this looks like a microphone. When the legal aid lawyer looks up, he looks ashamed, like he has forgotten something. Which, of course, he has. He has forgotten everything he learned in lawyer school. He has forgotten his two years spent articling with an important law firm, whose name he also forgets. He has forgotten the most crucial piece of advice he was given before coming to court this morning, which was that above and beyond all else, Judge McEchern hates ponytails on men. And to complicate matters completely, the legal aid lawyer has forgotten his own name, even though his initials are conveniently emblazoned in gold on his attaché case. But this latter forgetfulness seems unimportant at this moment, he thinks, because it seems incredibly unlikely that the very squinty old judge will ever ask him his name.

The legal aid lawyer looks at the judge.

The judge looks at the legal aid lawyer .

"Ahem. You with the ponytail," says Judge McEchern, pointing accusatively. "What's your name?"

SIDDHI

When Gregor Simpson awoke one morning from a night of restless dreams, he found himself transformed into a gigantic elephant.

This dream was so real Simpson grabbed for his nose and missed by two feet. He breathed a sigh of relief through two fairly human nostrils. Still suspicious, he felt for his ears and found the stiff cartilage and flabby lobes he'd grown accustomed to, and not, fortunately, big flappy hairy leathery things.

"Hm. What're you doing?" asked the sleepy figure next to him from under sky-blue sheets and a beige duvet.

"I was checking the size of my nose and ears," said Simpson helpfully, already swinging his legs out of bed.

"Oh," said the figure, inching over to the warmth left by Simpson. "And?"

"And all is normal."

"Hm . . . Greg?"

"Yeah?" Simpson now struggling into his jeans and pulling a T over his head.

"Now that your body parts are confirmed as regulation size, when can I meet your parents?"

"Give me time," said Simpson with what he hoped was a touch of irritation in his voice.

"We've been sleeping together for two years."

"Yeah, so?"

"So, we practically live together. Or I practically live here. Can I meet them soon, please?"

"Yeah, soon," said Simpson, leaning over to kiss the only strand of hair exposed from under the sheets and duvet. "Just give me time."

GANAPATI

But Your Honour, I stand before you, living proof that this homicide is not one.

If the son was murdered in a fit of jealous rage, a sort of reverse-Oedipal thing if you will, then the son would be dead and the father, indeed, guilty of homicide, sonicide, most particularly, me-icide.

But Your Honour, I stand before you.

I speak to you, somewhat nasally, perhaps (but wouldn't you if you had to talk through this enormous snout?).

All right, I grant you, he did take off my head, and there is that minor matter of the dead elephant, but he did ask permission before beheading the beast, and permission was duly granted. Granted, too, it took the entire volunteer fire department and then some to get his elephantine body from the river, but they did so in due course before decompositional elements could pollute the holy river, and I should add both my father and I feel deeply for Fireman Ephram Paglia and we hope he makes a hasty recovery from that nasty inguinal hernia. However. Homicide?

I submit to you that, being as I stand before you hale and hearty, albeit a mite uglier and somewhat more smelly than before, the only crime my dear father is guilty of is the unlawful disposal of a dead animal. I further submit the charges of murder, debasement of a body, and cruelty to animals be dropped and the sentence on the new charge be set at time served.

Let us be done with it.

Let's go have some milk.

SIDDHI

"So, what d'we have?" Delilah and Simpson are sitting at a red arborite table, cups of coffee and a box of timbits in front of them.

"Torso-less head, human; headless torso, elephant; blood samples."

"'Kay. What don't we have?"

"Human torso, elephant head, murder weapon, signs of struggle, footprints-fingerprints-other evidence of the murderer, body identification, motive, and probably some things I've forgot that we'll never get anyhow."

"Right. So where do we start?"

"Um. Timbit?"

Delilah ignores this. She is thinking about how everything about this case seems so abnormal and yet inextricably linked. It's like there is some sort of code they don't know how to read yet.

"Simpson, d'you know anyone in the East Indian community?"

"Soufayshn." Simpson looks like a chipmunk, a chocolate Timbit in one cheek and a cinnamon in the other.

"Say what?"

Simpson swallows. "South Asian. The community calls itself South Asian. At least the younger generation does."

"Okay. Well? Do you?"

"Hm? Oh, yeah. I know one or two guys. Want for me to check?"

Delilah shakes her head in amazement. How, she wonders, did Simpson make the detective grade? Boyish good looks and doughnut bondage, perhaps.

"Yes. I think that would be a splendid idea."

"Right," says Simpson, wiping chocolate bits from his mouth with a napkin. He leaves the table and heads over to the phone booth by the entrance. Delilah watches him call a memorized number and talk for a few seconds. Only then does he pull out a scrap of paper – actually, it's the same napkin he's just wiped his mouth with, Delilah notes – and begins scribbling furiously. He is on the phone for ten minutes. Delilah thinks she sees something in his face she has never seen before.

When Simpson returns, he tosses the napkin on to the table. Delilah picks up the napkin, covered on both sides with a scrawl. She can only make out a few letters here and there. The rest seems a series of commas, dashes, and half-formed script. She looks up at Simpson who, anxious to go, has not reseated himself.

"I can't read this," she says.

"Oh," says Simpson. "That's Forkner. Makes for quicker note-taking. You drive. I'll transcribe."

GANESH

I'm sitting here in my corner when I hear them coming up the steps, talking.

"Two days and nothing," she says.

"Uh-huh," he says.

"So who was it, anyway, who gave you all these Indian names?"

"South Asian names. A friend. I told you."

"Oh. Yeah."

The doorbell rings. I don't move. I hear Babiji rustling in the backroom and wonder if she will answer the door. I hope so. This sounds promising. The doorbell rings again and then I hear the *Aré va* from the backroom and Babiji comes rustling into the frontroom where I'm sitting. *Who could that be,* she asks herself or me, I'm not sure which, and runs to the door. *Who is it who is it?* The response from the voices outside is muffled owing to the great deal of noise Babiji makes as she unlatches and opens the door, rustling all the time, and now muttering to herself, *The police the police, what could they want?*

A man and woman walk in and introduce themselves as detectives Watson and Simpson. What excitement. I urge Babiji to seat them in the front room, which she does. This will be good. The woman speaks first.

"Mrs. Thakkar? We were wondering, that is, we were given your name by someone in the – South Asian community. . . ."

Babiji looks blank. She looks at the man for help. She looks over toward me but I stay silent. The woman tries to continue.

"The *South Asian* community."

Babiji still looks blank. *What this sowayzun?* she asks quietly.

The man speaks. "She means Indian," he says politely.

Ucha, says Babiji. *The Indian community*, and she smiles broadly as if she represents the whole.

The woman pulls out a photograph and as she passes it to Babiji, the window light reflects off the image and I catch a glimpse of that face. If I were a breathing, that is, animate, being, I would intake sharply.

"We were wondering if you know who this might be," says the woman. Babiji looks at the woman deeply before looking at the photograph. I can tell Babiji is warming to the woman. This is good. I like her too. Then Babiji looks at the photograph. Unlike me, she is a breather, so the sharp intake is possible for her. Babiji looks back at the woman. Babiji lowers her voice and says:

Evvin pachi avi gayoj. Rajo pachi avi gayoj. Vighnesvara rusto mahthi jenjeth hatari desey.

"Pardon?" says the woman.

"What she say?" says the man.

Ganeshji, says Babiji.

SIMPSON

Too close to home. This is all getting too close to home. Delilah really wants a break on this case. So do I, of course, but this is all too close to home.

And all because of that photograph of a beautiful sleeping prince, looking for a body that fit. Most of the folks we talked to looked blankly at the photograph. But then there was Mrs. Thakkar, who looked at the photograph and then looked up with such delight and triumph that Delilah actually took a step back. I don't know what she said. Something in Hindi, maybe Punjabi, I told Delilah. So, of course, she wants to get a Hindi/Punjabi translator out there. Do I know anyone? Well, yeah, kinda.

Too close to home.

'Gruesome' decapitation baffles police

FELIX DOLAN
Police Reporter

The head of a man in his 20s, discovered Tuesday in the river valley, has still not been identified and the remainder of his body has not been found.

Police say the head was discovered alongside animal remains by two people who were fishing in the area.

"We saw the head first," said John Hastings. "Then we saw this huge thing, an animal body. At first it looked like a whale, but then we thought it was a rhinoceros."

The animal remains are probably related to the decapitation in some manner, said Staff-Sergeant Henry Cooper, but would not identify the type of animal except to say it was very large, but not a rhinoceros.

Staff-Sergeant Cooper said city police are following leads in the East Indian community and are still investigating.

SIDDHI

"Delilah, this is Sandip. Sandip, my partner Delilah."

"Hi, nice ta meet ya."

"Same."

"Well, let's go."

"Sandip, this is Mrs. Thakkar. Mrs. Thakkar, Sandip Khosla."

Sandip, so good to see you. Where have you been hiding?

GANESH

They're back again. This time they've brought a nice Indian boy along. Very handsome. Some crooked teeth, but not entirely noticeable. Could use a haircut. Or else let it grow past his shoulders, then he'd look like a true prince, or maybe a rishi. Babiji knows this boy and she likes him a great deal, I can tell. They're speaking to Babiji.

"Can you ask her about the photograph?" asks the policeman. "I think she speaks Hindi. Maybe Punjabi."

The nice Indian boy asks her about the photograph, shows it to her again.

Tamay ghannah majana chokra cho. Ay tamari pasand nee chokri chay?

"Nahin, the photograph, ji."

Tamay punlayla cho?

"Nahin, do you recognize him?"

Evvin pachi avi gayoj. Rajo pachi avi gayoj. Vighnesvara rusto mahthi jenjeth hatari desey.

The Indian boy turns to his friends. "She's speaking Gujarati," he tells them.

"And?" asks the woman.

"And?" asks the man.

"And," says the Indian boy, "she says the prince has come home, that he's going to clear the path, something like that. I don't really speak Gujarati. Just know a bit from my grandmother."

"Who?"

"My grandmother, a Parsi from near Bombay."

"No, I mean who is this prince?"

"Oh, him. Ganesh. Or, rather, Vighnesvara, the avatar who is the lord of obstacles."

"Ganesh. Is he some Parsi god?"

"No, no, Hindu. Mrs. Thakkar is Hindu, too."

"And she's saying Ganesh has come, what, down to earth?"

"Well, no, not really. See, he's always been here, always been right —"

The Indian boy's eyes sweep across the room. I try to be small because it's not polite to garner too much attention, but he sees me anyway. I try to smile a welcome but they don't appear to notice. My stomach growls a bit — I'm always nervous meeting new people — but they ignore this, too. He points at me and all eyes are on me.

"— right there."

SIDDHI

"Well, Sandip, thanks for your help."

"Yeah, thanks."

"No problem. I hope this will be of some use."

"Hard to say right now, but we'll see."

"Yeah, we'll see."

"Okay, see ya later, Sandip."

"Yeah, goodbye, it was nice to meet you."

"Right. Bye Delilah. Bye Greg."

"Bye."

"Bye."

"*Greg?*"

JUDGE McECHERN

"All rise."

Everybody rises.

Judge McEchern peers around the corner of the door to his chambers. He sees the Crown Prosecutor, preparing for the day by tugging at her collar. He sees the legal aid lawyer shuffling through papers importantly. He sees the gallery, made up of the usual contingent of lowlifes, foreigners, and a few others. But there is no elephant.

Judge McEchern strides in and climbs up the three stairs to his judge table. Today will be a better day, he thinks to himself. Today will be fine.

"Good morning," he says to his clerk, to the Crown Prosecutor, to the legal aid lawyer, to the gallery, and they all nod or mumble good morning back.

"I see there's no elephant in my courtroom today," says Judge McEchern smugly.

There is an undefinable silence in the courtroom. This is the silence people make when someone in the room farts, thinks Judge McEchern. As he has not heard anyone fart, and he has surely not farted himself, Judge McEchern surmises people are making silence on account of his statement. He remembers being told, when he was a young piano student, that if he made a mistake during a recital he should make the same mistake at least two more times so the audience thinks this is intentional.

"Yes sir, no elephant in my courtroom today," says Judge McEchern, a bit louder this time.

If this were a piano recital, Judge McEchern thinks, the audience would not be fooled.

"Uh, is there an elephant in the courtroom today?"

The Crown Prosecutor stands, leaves her collar alone for a moment.

"No, your Worship, there is no – elephant – in the courtroom today." She pauses and looks around the courtroom as if to make sure.

"Should there be?"

Judge McEchern checks to make sure his gavel is in its place. It is. That's because he has been wishing so hard for a gavel like they have on American TV that when he was shopping for tile caulking for his downstairs bathroom at his favourite giant hardware store and he noticed their advertising display featuring a wrinkly old man in flowing black robes brandishing a cheap but solid wooden gavel, well, Judge McEchern just couldn't resist slipping that item into a pocket in his twenty-year-old down-filled coat.

He picks up the gavel and bangs it twice, quite hard, on the bench.

"Court will recess," says Judge McEchern, "for lunch."

JUDGE McECHERN

Judge McEchern sits at his judge table, his chin slumped in his hand. He is listening to some woman named Mrs. Thakkar talk in a language he does not understand. She obviously enjoys telling this very long story, but Judge McEchern does not understand a bit of it, save for a few words of English Mrs. Thakkar appears to throw in for no apparent reason.

Mrs. Thakkar gesticulates wildly and her eyes grow large and her voice gets big. Then she becomes very sombre and her face softens and her voice gets small. She cups her hands in front of her, then spreads them apart so far Judge McEchern thinks she will do herself an injury.

She talks on and on and on.

Mrs. Thakkar has been called as a witness for the defence.

The legal aid lawyer sits at his desk, smiling, nodding so vigorously sometimes that Judge McEchern can see that microphone-like ponytail bobbing up and down.

Judge McEchern does not like this.

After what must be an interminable time, Mrs. Thakkar's voice lowers and she is silent. The legal aid lawyer rises.

"Thank you, Mrs. Thakkar," he says. "I have no further questions."

The Crown Prosecutor half-rises and says, half-tugging at her collar, "No questions," and seats herself.

Judge McEchern is suddenly very alert. And hostile.

"What is the meaning of this?" trumpets Judge McEchern, glaring at the legal aid lawyer. "I didn't understand a bloody word she said, you sit there grinning like a jackass and nodding so hard your bloody ponytail threatens to fly off into the ceiling, and *you*," he shouts over at the collar-tugging Crown Prosecutor, "you have no questions. How the hell could you have questions when, I'm assuming, you didn't understand a bloody word she said either?"

There is a vein in Judge McEchern's neck that is now very purple.

"Now," says Judge McEchern, leaning back in his judge chair and promising himself he shouldn't get so riled next time, "will the Indian translator please tell me what she said?"

Eyes shuffle nervously.

"I said, will the translator *please* tell me what she said?"

Judge McEchern waits for an answer and then looks around the courtroom. He sees a lot of foreign faces, but none rise to speak. He feebly asks, "*Is* there an Indian translator in the courtroom?"

He expects no answer and is therefore surprised when the legal aid lawyer rises. .

"Well," says the legal aid lawyer, "I do speak Hindi and Punjabi."

"So what did she say?"

"Well," says the legal aid lawyer, "the trouble is Mrs. Thakkar's mother tongue is Gujarati."

"I see. And do you, Mr. Khosla, speak Goojraddy?"

"Well, not really. But I understand it quite well. You see, my grandmother, she was a Parsi from near Bombay, and she used to tell us stories, Hindu stories mostly, but some about Zoroaster —"

"Mr. Khosla. If you do, indeed, understand Goojraddy, and Mrs. Thakkar's mother tongue is, indeed, Goojraddy, would you be so kind as to translate what she has just so generously shared with the court?"

Judge McEchern smiles sweetly.

The legal aid lawyer smiles sweetly back.

"Well," he says, "for reasons I have yet to determine, Mrs. Thakkar decided to give her testimony in her father's tongue, Tamil, to be precise."

The legal aid lawyer begins to sit down, then pops to his feet as if he has just remembered something.

"Your Honour, I don't understand Tamil."

Judge McEchern crosses his hands in front of him on his judge table and purses his lips.

"I never want to have this happen again in my courtroom," he says, so softly that the court stenographer has to ask him to repeat himself. "Is that understood?" He does not wait for an answer. He will get through this case before it kills him, he thinks to himself. He looks over at the witness box and sees that Mrs. Thakkar is beaming up at him. Apparently she likes him, although the feelings are clearly not mutual. He tells Mrs. Thakkar she is excused, something she apparently understands quite well, and she totters off the stand and back into the gallery.

"Does the defence have any more witnesses before we adjourn for the weekend?" asks Judge McEchern without looking up and hoping beyond hope the legal aid lawyer will say he has no more witnesses.

However, this is not to be. The legal aid lawyer says he has one more witness before the weekend adjournment and he spouts off some very long very foreign-sounding name.

Judge McEchern is quite content to coast through the afternoon without once looking up at the despicable people in this despicable courtroom. But, resolute in this as he may be, he finds his head unwillingly rising up when he hears what is an unmistakable snort.

At the back of the courtroom, ambling forward to take the witness stand, is a pot-bellied, bow-legged, brown-skinned man with an elephant's head where his own should be.

from CDOR, your country listening station

POLICE HAVE FOUND PARTS OF A MAN'S BODY AND SOME UNIDENTIFED ANIMAL REMAINS IN THE RIVER VALLEY. THE DECAPITATED BODY WAS THAT OF AN EAST INDIAN MAN WHO HAS NOT YET BEEN IDENTIFIED. POLICE ARE LOOKING FOR THE KILLER OR KILLERS WHO MIGHT HAVE DUMPED THE BODY BEFORE ESCAPING BY BOAT. ANYONE WHO SAW ANYTHING SUSPICIOUS YESTERDAY EVENING SHOULD CONTACT THE POLICE.

–30–

VIGHNESVARA

Being this lord of obstacles, among other things, makes for some quiet confusion. Ha. Quiet. Hmph. See, folks put my "altar" ego on every windowsill, coffee-table, podium, street-corner, bedpost, temple entrance, bedroom shrine, car dashboard, baseball cap, tie-dye shirt, underwear even, and still no one can figure out if I'm here to place obstacles in their way or to remove them. Least of all me. Sometimes, I think, I do both at the same time. Being lord of obstacles is fun, but a lot of work, I tell ya. Ha.

Elephants like that, more so if they're elephant gods.

Elephants, colonized into indentured labour, lifting, moving, shifting, heaving logs and trees and rocks for the satisfaction of human desire.

Elephants, big, immovable, resistentialists, bigger buttresses than a concrete cul-de-sac.

47

GANESH

I am on late-night television.

I've been lots of places in thousands of years but I've never been on late-night television.

I'm sitting by the host's desk. This particular version of me is three feet tall, wooden, carved, sculpted with carpentry tools. My trunk is tucked inside the folds of wood by my chest. I feel soft tonight. And thirsty.

The host is an ironic character with bad teeth. I notice the teeth of others a lot. Sometimes they notice my teeth, my tusk, singular, but more often they don't.

"We have a special treat for ya tonight," the host says, grinning wildly. "Tonight we're going to introduce you to the elephant god of the hindoos, Ganesh. Now, some of you might have heard that Ganesh idols around the world have taken to drinking milk."

There is scattered laughter.

"That's right, you heard me right. Stone, brass, and wooden idols are actually behaving like pussycats and drinking milk."

More laughter, less scattered.

"But before I introduce you to Ganesh" – he looks down at me – "you don't mind waiting, do you?" and I shake my wooden head, but so imperceptibly that the host doesn't notice and the television viewers will mistake this for camera shake – "I'm going to bring out the owner of this particular Ganesh-god, a Mr. Ravvy Guppta. Mr. Guppta?"

There is applause, polite, and the curtain to the left of the host parts and my friend, a slight man of about fifty-five, takes tiny steps out into the bright lights and edges over to the host. The bad-teethed host grabs the guest's hand and shakes it vigorously exactly three times, then lets it drop. The guest sits down.

"So, Mr. Guppta, can I call you Ravvy?"

"Certainly, but actually, it's Ravi, Ravi Gupta. The Indian 'a' is short, sounds like 'uh'." Ravi Gupta always keeps his lips tightly curled even when he talks so it's hard to tell what sort of teeth he has, but I have seen him laughing often so I know his teeth are pretty good.

"Sure, okay, Ruvvie then, Ruvvie, can you tell us a bit about this phenomenon?" When the host says "phenomenon" he puts his hands up by his ears and flicks his middle and index fingers up and down, placing his head in quotation marks, bad teeth and all.

"Yes, well, it all started about a year ago. Ganesh, as you have said, is the elephant-headed Hindu deity. Many people keep representations of him in their homes and make offerings of milk and sweets to him."

"Must be good to be a god, eh, Ruvvie?"

There is laughter on cue. I don't particularly like this talk-show host's irreverence but he is, after all, quite right. It is good to be a god.

"Must be. Anyway, about a year ago a boy was born in India, and they said he was born with the head of an elephant, that he was, in fact, the god Ganesh born into this world."

"Sort of like a second elephant coming? Or would that be an elephant coming again?"

More laughter. But I notice a few people in the audience take on a sullen look.

"Something like that. The phenomenon you talk about, though, is what has happened since then. All over the world, representations of Ganesh have actually been drinking the milk offered to them."

"Drinking the milk, eh? Do they munch on the sweets, too, heh heh. Too many sweets and you know what that means, eh? A trip to the god-dentist. To fill in those holy cavities."

I find this quite funny and I chortle. Here I am, one-tusked and all, and here's this very odd host with a bad case of dental neglect, and he's making teeth jokes. Very funny. Very funny indeed. The host hears me chortle and looks down momentarily, then looks back at his guest.

"Ravvie, before we do a live demonstration, I'd like to bring out another guest. *Ann*-il *Sush*-eli is a physicist and writer, his last book is called *Hard Questions and Easy Answers in Everyday Living* and he's here with us tonight. *Ann*-il?"

From the same break in the curtains appears a tall, well-dressed man with close-cropped hair and a big smile. He is about thirty-five and his teeth are perfect. When he gets closer I realize that at least three of his teeth are capped, but whoever did the dental work had a good eye for matching colour so it hardly shows.

"Welcome back, *Ann*-il."

"Thanks," says Anil, smiling broadly and reaching out to shake Ravi's hand. He shakes it vigorously exactly three times and then lets it drop. Ravi, who has risen to shake the new guest's hand, finds himself shuffled over one seat so that Anil can sit next to the host.

"So, *Ann*-il. You're a physicist and a writer, and you just so happen to write about everyday things," says the host, doing the finger-flapping, head-quoting bit when he says "everyday things." "Tell our audience what you make of this milk-drinking phenomenon."

"It's really very simple," says Anil, furrowing his brow. "It all has to do with surface tension and liquid viscosity. You see, if you bring a small amount of liquid, say, on a spoon, in contact with something solid – well, here, let me show you." He starts to pull items out of his jacket and begins talking quicker and I soon lose interest. I begin to look around. ". . . take this coffee stir stick and . . ."

I look over at Ravi Gupta. Part of me, the part that stands wooden and carved up on this soundstage, has lived with him for twenty-two years. He is a very good man. He greets me every morning and every evening except when he and his wife and two daughters go on vacation for three weeks every summer.

". . . small amount of liquid in the spoon . . ."

The Gupta family keeps me in a corner, always with lots to look at and eat. Sometimes the two young girls put silvery garlands around my neck which makes me feel very proud. They were the first ones I took milk from and I remember how big their eyes got and how they ran from the room to tell mummy and daddy. Ravi Gupta did everything late in life. He got a career late. He got married late. He had children late. He was a late person.

". . . the surface tension of the milk . . ."

The milk? I suddenly remember I'm still thirsty. This Anil character has milk somewhere. I start paying attention.

"And so you see, no miracle, just plain and simple physics."

There is a small amount of applause but the audience is losing interest. The host knows this and tries to intervene.

"Very interesting, *Ann*-il. But we decided to conduct our own experiment, which is why we have Ravvie Guppta on the show, along with his very own elephant god. Ravvie, if you would be so kind as to lift the idol up to the table so he's within camera shot —"

This, Ravi does, lifts me up onto the host's table. It was hot on the floor, but up here I get the full blast of the TV lights. My wooden skin, even oiled as it is, feels like it's ready to crack. I do not like this. The lights are not just hot, but bright, ten times brighter than the sun that finds its way through the south window to my corner at home. This is too much. I hear the host prattling on but I'm not paying attention. It's hot. Too hot. I need a drink. Badly. I see a woman appear from the break in the curtains. She is dressed in what appears to be a sequined one-piece bathing suit. She reflects the TV lights with her sequins, her blonde-blonde hair, and her exceptionally white teeth. She has the best set of teeth I have seen tonight, even including Anil's. I think I have seen her before, yes, I have, on TV, she's the one who does all those Dairy Commission ads, the ones which make me very thirsty. I remember the way she gulps the milk now, the way she smiles after and how her white-white teeth gleam. She is carrying something with her. She brings it to a decorative table by the curtain, a long way away, at least twenty feet from where I sit. It is a jug, a huge glass jug, full of frothy milk! It is so heavy it wobbles as she goes about opening the lid and beginning to pour. I can almost taste it. But, what's this, she's pouring the tiniest of amounts into a little ceramic dish. Why, that's hardly enough for a taste. I need a drink, a real draught, not a pathetic sprinkling like that. She leaves the jug on the decorative table and walks over to me with the little dish of milk. She is smiling, smiling, and her teeth fill up my vision and the audience is laughing and applauding and the host is laughing and Anil is laughing and she comes right up to me, bends over with that tiny dish and holds it to my buried trunk.

We, goddesses and gods that is, are under the strictest orders not to make a show of ourselves. Let people believe what they will, we are told, just don't go out of our way to put on a song and dance number. People are so gullible, we are told, that even the slightest godly act will cause them to prostrate and pray and babble for years to come. Not worth it, we're told. Act our age, we're told.

But it is truly hot up here. And the amount of milk being offered by this blonde sequined toothy Dairy Commission woman is pathetic indeed. There, just a few feet away, just a trunk's throw, is a whole jug of refreshing milk. A whole jug.

I forget myself.

I forget I am made of wood.

I forget I am on national television.

I forget I am supposed to behave like a silent god.

I do not forget that I am Ganesha, lord of obstacles. Currently, there is a silly little ceramic bowl of milk, a blonde sequined perfect-toothed advertising queen, and a twenty-foot gap impeding my path to the object of my desire.

I unravel my nose. I can hear the grumbly sounds of wood fibre letting go of itself. I squiggle my nose, free at last, free at last, thank Shiv-almighty, I'm free at last.

My trunk swings free as it has before, way before. My trunk unrolls, unstiffens, languishes itself out and far away. My trunk gently flicks the ceramic bowl out of offering hands onto soundstage floor, crack-crack, droplets spill. No sense in crying.

My trunk furls around sequined tummy, brings in memories of snake-friends and full bellies, gently lifts blonde body and sets her aside, she gawking now, teeth gnashing in silent scream.

My trunk unfurls from tummy and is indian rubber: reaches out, out stretch, stretches long, longs forward, forwards bend, bends time, times across the gap and touches tips teeters and the jug of milk wobbles and tilts and off it goes, a great explosion of frothy milk and broken glass, splinters and droplets everywhere, my trunk goes crazy, vacuuming up the liquidy spots, soothing, cooling milk!

There is absolute quiet in the room. At first, when I pulled out my trunk, there was an audible gasp or two. Now there is nothing. Absolute silence. Stillness. The only sound is that of my errant trunk, a mind of its own, still sucking and lapping at the spilled milk.

This is not good.

This is national television.

This is going to be a long and convoluted story.

I pull my trunk back, truculently tuck it back in my wooden chest.

I open my mouth a titch. Perhaps I should explain.

I burp.

Hijinx highlight sweeps week

HENRIETTA SCHMALL
Entertainment Columnist

Unexpected things happen on live late-night television.

And the fact that more unexpected things happen during sweeps week is purely coincidental if we are to believe network producers.

Here's what's happened so far in this crucial week which determines the network's share of the viewers:

• Callie, a secondary character on the popular sitcom *Family Circles*, has a baby—in itself, not unusual and also not likely to grab the headlines. So the network execs decided to boost their audience share by promoting a live birth on television. That's right, while the show was being broadcast a TV crew walked into Mercy General and started taping away in a delivery room. "This gives our audiences the feeling of being in a real birthing process," says **Jay Sneed**, one of the ABC honchos. No doubt.

• *Newswatch*, the crime-hyped CBS late night investigative news show, has host **Peter Gross** shivering outside Attica prison on a death watch, waiting for the execution news of serial killer **Clem Pallor**, explaining to his viewers that a democratic system would allow the live broadcast of executions.

• And NBC's *Late Night*, not to be outdone, has American Dairy Commission model **Sandy Springer** serving a cup of milk to a statue of the Hindu elephant god, only to have the statue "come alive" and wave his obviously string-operated trunk around the stage. Executive producer **Norm Wiener** claims, however, that none of this was planned, and that the statue actually did "come alive." Sure, Norm, sure. How are the ratings?

VIGHNESVARA

"The court calls Ganesh also known as Ganesha also known as Vighnesvara also known as Lord of Obstacles also known as Ganapati also known as Buddhi also known as Lord of Wisdom also known as Siddhi also known as Lord of Desire also known as Ganeshji also known as the Elephant God also known as the Elephant-headed One also known as Lord of Propitious Beginnings also known as Lord of Written Projects to the stand."

The aforementioned lumbers to the witness stand, holds up a pudgy hand.

"Are you Ganesh also known as Ganesha also known as Vighnesvara also known as Lord of Obstacles also known as Ganapati also known as Buddhi also known as Lord of Wisdom also known as Siddhi also known as Lord of Desire also known as Ganeshji also known as the Elephant God also known as the Elephant-headed One also known as Lord of Propitious Beginnings also known as Lord of Written Projects?"

"Yes."

"Do you, Ganesh also known as Ganesha also known as Vighnesvara also known as Lord of Obstacles also known as Ganapati also known as Buddhi also known as Lord of Wisdom also known as Siddhi also known as Lord of Desire also known as Ganeshji also known as the Elephant God also known as the Elephant-headed One also known as Lord of Propitious Beginnings also known as Lord of Written Projects swear to tell the truth, the whole truth, and nothing but the truth, so help you god?"

The elephant-headed one looks somewhat curiously at the proffered Bible, then shrugs an elephantine shrug, and puts his hand on the book.

"I do."

JUDGE McECHERN

Judge McEchern is at home in his den. He is sitting in his favourite chair, staring straight ahead. He is playing that mental game where he tells himself to try not to think about elephants. But of course, just like the game is supposed to show, everytime he tries not to think about elephants he winds up thinking about elephants. Particularly elephants in his courtroom.

Sometimes Judge McEchern thinks the only place he is safe from elephants is in his den, as long as he doesn't try not to think about elephants.

Judge McEchern slouches in his favourite chair. He is dressed in a nightgown and a pair of faded green boxer shorts. In his left hand is a crystal snifter of very fine cognac. This is his second healthy helping of what will eventually number eight. In his right hand is his lifeline to the world. He clicks the ∧ button and hears and sees his world change from droning monotone voices to rich clear operatic notes; from flickering blues and reds to even-toned yellows.

Judge McEchern is channel-surfing.

He tells no one about his penchant for channel-surfing.

He tells everyone that he despises television, that it is the ruin of contemporary civilization.

Clickclick.

holy roller singing damnation for everybody click *soft as a baby's bottom* clickclick *twenty-four hour news and weather scrolling across the screen* click *a blue-clad hockey player tips the puck past a sprawling goaltender c'est le but says the announcer* click *quake in china today very serious news announcer* clickclickclick *cackling talkshow host munch on the sweets too heh heh* click *movie of the week woman run-*

ning in dark clickclick *stupid standup routine ha ha* clickclick *i do not understand says lieutenant data.*

Judge McEchern concurs.

When that newspaper interviewed him two years ago, Judge McEchern couldn't say enough about the filth and degradation on television these days. All this violence and sex, he told the reporter, glorified by those rock videos and even the news shows. Did he watch television himself? she asked. Never, he said. Hardly ever. Wouldn't permit one in his house. Well, his son had one in his room but only for educational programs and the occasional video. The bane of our existence, he said.

Click.

Judge McEchern takes a swallow of his cognac. He used to like the way cognac smelled and the way it put a warm feeling on his tongue. Now he just notices the slight burn in his throat. He clicks.

woman now talking to police movie of the week click *hockey between periods* clickclickclickclick *smiling model in tight bathing suit* clickclick *commercial for body deodorant* clickclickclick *same stupid standup routine* click *smiling model in tight bathing suit holding a tiny saucer* click.

Click back.

Judge McEchern sets the remote control down on the arm of his chair. The model is smiling wider now and the camera zooms in to her face. Judge McEchern's arm slides onto his leg. Voices in the background make the model laugh and her earlobes bob up and down and her lips glow red. Judge McEchern's hand moves up his thigh. The model makes her way over to the talkshow host's table. She is walking carefully so as not to spill whatever is in the saucer. Judge McEchern squints a bit and lets his hand slip inside his boxer shorts. The model turns to the camera and smiles again. Her teeth are brilliant and set off just so by that lipstick. Judge McEchern explores with his hand, searches around, grabs. She lifts the saucer up to the lips of a little statue. She holds the saucer with both hands. Judge McEchern thinks of her hands and her lips and he pretends the statue's lips are his lips. Judge McEchern begins to squeeze and release, squeeze and release, as rhythmically as a judge his age can be expected. He closes his eyes for a moment, then opens them to see what she is doing now. Something has knocked the saucer from her hand. He squeezes and releases faster. Her mouth is open in surprise. Squeezesqueezesqueeze. She rises from the ground. She is floating. Oh squeezesqueeze. No, she is not floating. Someone, some thing has picked her up. The camera pulls back. Judge McEchern recognizes the statue, recognizes its head, recognizes its trunk, now firmly wrapped around the model's waist, all at once. Judge McEchern's mouth opens wide. He squeezes very hard, automatically. Too hard. Judge McEchern forgets where he is. This is not his courtroom and he is not holding his gavel. Therefore, he should not be doing what he is doing, which is squeezingsqueezing as tight as his slightly arthritic but unfortunately strong and vise-like hands are capable of. And, as the elephant's trunk winds across the TV screen and topples a tall glass jug of milk, Judge McEchern should not be banging his gavel on his bench, two times, hard, to make it all stop.

Click.

SIDDHI

When Gregor Simpson awoke one morning after a night of restless dreams, he had been transformed into a brown man.

This dream was so real Simpson leapt out of bed, cracked his knee on the gold-lettered attaché case by the door, and crunched his nose into the bathroom mirror in his haste to see what colour his skin was.

"What's it this time," said the still figure from under tan sheets and a beige duvet.

"I dwemt I hab tuhned into a bwown man," said Simpson.

"Uh-hm. And?"

"An' den I hit my knee on yaw bwiefcase."

"And?"

"An' when I wuz in da bat'woom I hid by dose on da miwwa."

"You should know by now, Greg," said the figure, still under cover of sheet and duvet, "brown men aren't that clumsy."

DELILAH

Greg. He called him Greg. Nobody calls Simpson Greg. Not even his mother. Hmph. His mother. I'd only met his mother once and there was something strange even then. We dropped in on his parents one time when we had to travel north for some court stuff. Here was Simpson, bringing home a woman without a hint of explanation, none of this "This is the woman I work with," or nothing and not a question from either mother or father. As if this was an everyday occurrence. "Oh, hello Gregor, nice of you to come for dinner, who's your friend, Delilah, is it, well, that's nice, hello Delilah, please sit down, we're having fish, I hope that's okay."

I asked him later if he had talked to his parents about me and he said nope, never talked with them about work, and I figure, okay, then, what about other things, personal things, and he said, yeah, some personal stuff came up, but that they didn't seem to be interested. Not interested. I've never known of any parents to be not interested in their only child's day-to-day existence. Something funny was going on with that family.

And now this.

See ya, Greg. Bye, Greg. Catchya later, Greg.

Greg Greg Greg. Who was this Sandip?

Oh. I see a penny dropping. A nickel. A dime, a quarter, a mound of silver dollars.

Oh. Greg. Oh.

Police seek gang suspects in beheading

FELIX DOLAN
Police Reporter

City police have made no arrests in a gang-related murder in which the victim's severed head was left beside an elephant carcass.

The head of an East Indian male was found by two fishermen last week in the river valley.

Staff-Sergeant Henry Cooper said yesterday police were close to making an arrest but declined to comment on whether the killing was gang-related.

Decapitation of the victim is a common form of revenge in South Asian gang warfare, according to a Toronto criminologist.

In an exclusive interview, Dr. Bea Sandath told The Star that Indian criminals who immigrate to Canada often find themselves reconnected to tribal gang members, many who are themselves fleeing Indian justice.

"I don't want to perpetuate stereotypes," said Dr. Sandath, "but for many of these people their gang allegiances are of a ritual nature, tying them to their rural roots in India and East Africa."

"It's in their blood."

"The machete is the weapon of choice and the decapitation serves as a warning to others who might betray gang confidences," she added.

Dr. Sandath said she did not know why elephant remains might be found at the scene but speculated that it had something to do with a type of sacrifice.

MR. S

I told ya. I was workin'. All evening. Okay, then, one more
time, but that's it, 'kay? My name is Sam Sribhaiman.
Everyone calls me Mr. S. Makes things easier for the anglo
tongue. I teach at the U, classics department. Well, not really classics anymore cuz they changed the name, now it's
Asian Studies. But I teach mythology, mostly Vedic stuff,
though I can do most anything 'round the Indian subconti-
nent, y'know? Like Hindu cosmology, those 300 million
names of god, y'know, Buddhism also, and stuff around the
Moguls too, though I try to stay away, more or less, from just
the straight history stuff, eh? So, yeah, that's why I have that
shiv, or rather had it i guess, cuz god knows where it's got
to. But I didn't use it to kill anyone, 'kay? Jeez. Got it on a
trip to India, a research and teaching gig. Y'know, one of
those five-week tours of the holy land an' all. Me an' two
other profs, one from religious studies, one from history, an'
about twenty-five students. We toured around a bit, visited a
lot of these universities in the south, Mysore, an' all.
Anyway, it was at a temple, 'bout thirty clicks outside of
Mysore that I got the shiv. This guy, thought he was a snake
charmer cuz he was just sitting by the road on the way up to
the temple, hailin' folks passin' by. Anyways, I was a bit
behind the others, needed my own space, dig, an' you'd know
what I mean if you'd spent the past three weeks with a buncha mostly spoiled Canadian Indophiles. So, like, I'm hangin'
back and this guy calls me over, starts off in English like he
does with everyone else, "Saab, come here, come here please,"
this sorta thing, then switches over to Tamil, kinda mixing
in Hindi, and we start talkin' like this, findin' enough com-

mon words in English Tamil Hindi for us ta understand each other, see? Anyway, so then he reaches into this bag, this dirty muslin thing, the same sort of weave the snakecharmers use to keep their sickly toothless cobras in, so that's what I figure he's got, but he pulls out this huge, and I mean huge, sheathed shiv. No shit. Anyways, looks like it's from outta a museum or somethin' but I could peg this guy right away as someone who wasn't gonna walk into a museum and out with this gigantic artifact, like that's just not the way things work over there. So we talk a bit, Hindi Tamil English, and he tells me I could take the sword, I mean just take it, and promise to protect it. Started saying how Lord Shiva had entrusted the sword to him and how he was gettin' sick and had to pass it on. No shit, just like something outta an ol knight's tale or something. But it's true. So I take it and bring it back home. That's the story.

So I've had it ever since, that is, until a coupla weeks ago. I was sitting in my office, playin' on the computer, doin' searches for stuff around Shiva as a matter of fact, when there's this knock at my door. I look up and there's this woman, and this is the freaky part, cuz when I first sees her I'm pretty sure I know her and I say "hi" in that way you say hi when yer greetin' an ol' friend. And that's when I notice that I don't really know this woman, haven't ever met her, and then I'm lookin at her and I figure she's about twenty-five and then like I'm hallucinatin' she suddenly changes and looks like she's about eighty-five and the only thing that stays the same about her are her eyes which are dark and just seem to know ya, y'know?

"You Dr. Sribhaiman?" she asks.

An' I say, yeah, that's me, though I'm real nervous and I can't figure out why.

"Parvati," she says. Not like, "I'm Parvati," or "Hi, my name's Parvati," just "Parvati," which sounds less like an introduction than, well, this sounds stupid, but an invocation. So much so I don't even know if, like, she's telling me that's her name or what? And then I figure out what's so odd, why I'm so freaked. This woman, she's standing outside my office, and she has this sorta half-smile on, not like she's laughing or nuthin, or even happy, just like that's the way she always looks, and then I think, I don't know why, I wonder what her teeth look like, and I realize that through this all, her saying "You Dr. Sribhaiman," and stating "Parvati" like that and all, I haven't seen her teeth and that's cuz she hasn't once opened her mouth. I swear.

GANESH

I'm standing on Aijaz Ahmad's *In Theory: Class Nations Literatures*. Off to my right is *Exotic Parodies* by Asha Varadharajan. Next to that is a well-thumbed version of *British India Before 1857* written by some Brigadier General whose name I can't read from here. Peripherally, tucked into the pages of a hardcover coffee-table type book about the Raj, I can see a highlighted and underlined version of an article by Gayatri Spivak. I am up to my sandalwood butt in theories of postcoloniality and subalternity. I never get to read more than a page at a time of any given theoretical text, though, whatever stuff Sam leaves open and in my line of vision, either right underfoot on my shelf, or over on the corner of his desk. Sometimes he leaves it open to a particularly difficult or important passage – he does that with Spivak a lot. But sometimes he just leaves it open when he has to rush out for an appointment or a class or gets interrupted by a phone call or a visitor, usually a young undergraduate. From where I stand I get a good view of the door, so I usually see the apprehensive undergrads before Sam does. They stand there nervously, mouse-like, hoping some sort of divine intervention will cause Sam to look up from his work. I try sending Sam telepathic messages, urging him to look up. If that doesn't work, and it rarely does, I send telepathic messages to the student, trying to convince her or him that a little knock on the open door isn't going to cause the heavens to come crashing down. But they're usually too nervous to knock and so they stand there, sometimes for ages. The record is four minutes and seventeen seconds, when this second-year guy stood there swallowing, shifting his weight from one foot to the other, making sighing noises, but very softly, so although I could hear him, Sam couldn't. Many of the undergraduates who visit Sam have a crush on him. He doesn't notice these things. Lots of students think he notices these things and is just too suave to care. But the truth is he just doesn't know. Sam is not aware that he is attractive. Sam is not aware that about half the undergraduates who visit his office, men and women, have minor to major crushes on him. Sam is not aware that he is a sexual being.

When she comes to Sam's office, we recognize each other immediately, of course. I am very happy she has come by. She seems quite pleased to see me, too. We chat, reminisce, talk about what we've been up to the last little while. I talk about the critical theory I've been piecing together, one page at a time, and she talks about a very serious problem she has, which is why she's here. We do this in the two-and-a-half seconds she is standing at Sam's door, he not noticing her. I tell her she should knock unless she wants to wait another two-hundred-fifty-five seconds and go for a record. She's had enough of records, she says. She needs some results. She knocks, self-assuredly, so that when Sam looks up he knows he will not be greeting a first-year student, although it might be a major in Asian Studies or a graduate student, because they knock with more confidence. Professors do not knock, they just hang onto the door frame with one hand and lean in so far that their rear foot lifts off the ground and they look like overweight and aging ballerinas and they say, "Hey, Sam."

But when Sam looks up he knows he is not greeting a major in Asian Studies or a graduate student or a pudgy prof.

"You Dr. Sribhaiman?"

"Uh. Oh. Yeah, uh-huh."

"Parvati."

from CDOR, *your country listening station*

POLICE ARE REFUSING TO DISMISS CLAIMS THAT
LAST WEEK'S BIZARRE DISCOVERY OF A MAN'S
HEAD IN A PILE OF ELEPHANT REMAINS IS GANG-
RELATED. NO ARRESTS HAVE BEEN MADE BUT
RCMP HAVE QUESTIONED SEVERAL KNOWN EAST
INDIAN GANG MEMBERS IN CONNECTION WITH THE
MURDER. A MAN'S SEVERED HEAD WAS DISCOV-
ERED IN THE RIVER VALLEY LAST WEEK. THE BODY
HAS NOT BEEN FOUND.

–30–

VIGHNESVARA

I'm hanging with Simpson and Delilah. They don't know I'm hanging with them, but I am. Never can tell when folks can do with the removal or replacement of an obstacle or two. They've been moving quite handily with this case but I have a feeling it's time to lend a hand or they'll never come to the end.

They're having coffee together. Along with a box of tiny donut things. At a red arborite table. They're focussed on each other intensely, no doubt working on the case.

"So were you ever going to tell me?"

"Tell you what?"

"You know. About Sandip. About you."

"What about me?"

"You're just trying to make me say it."

"Say what?"

"See! You're doing it again."

"Doing what again."

"Trying to get me to say you're – you're –"

"Can't say it, can ya?"

"That you're y'know, like, gay. Okay?"

"Okay."

"Well?"

"What?"

"Well, I'm your partner. Don't you think you should've told me? I mean, I'd have understood. I do understand. We talk, don't we? We tell each other things."

"What, like *I'm, y'know, like, gay, okay?* Look, D, you're my partner and my friend, yeah, maybe even my best friend, but if even you can't get out the words, if even you start looking

ONCE UPON AN ELEPHANT

at me differently just cuz you find out I'm gay, how d'ya think the guys are gonna react?"

"Well. They'd understand."

"Understand, yeah, right, like they'd understand me in the back alley outside of the 10-4 Club. Or understand me in the locker room. They'd understand."

"Simpson. They're not like that."

"No? Then how are they like?"

"Well, okay, maybe they are like that. But I'm not. You could have told me."

"It's not that simple, D. It's not that simple. This may be a big city, but it's a small community, y'know? Most everyone knows everybody or knows of everybody. And me, a cop, D, I can't be out."

"And your parents?"

"Straight, as far I know."

"No, I mean, do they know?"

"Well, I've never told 'em I'm gay, if that's what ya mean. But, then, you ever told your parents you're straight? You are straight, aren't you?"

Talk talk talk. All this talk. Who's doing what to whom, who knows about it, how it's done. Sexuality this and sexual that. How-to manuals, help books, phone lines, chat-lines. These people don't need my help with obstacles. They're too busy moving them around for themselves. And to think I once thought the friezes at Khujurao were complicated. Anyway, what's the problem here? Sandip's a very nice boy and he and this Simpson seem to fit well together. I suppose there's that problem of cultural differences. I remember that time I brought back my very first consort and how Parvati flashed with goddess anger. "This just isn't right, Ganeshji," she sputtered. "A boy like you should have a consort, very true, but this? Why, this is a demon, a dweller of the underworld. And we're gods. Our types just don't mix. And if you won't think of your poor mother, then think of yourselves. Whatever would the children look like?" Of course, she came around when she realized that, while her son's consort might indeed have the body of a snake, her son himself had an elephant's head, so none of this purity shmurity stuff. But I'm digressing badly. Back to Simpson and Delilah. Someone else is joining them, a young man dressed in black, carrying what appears to be a tiny lock of hair in a ponytail. No, my mistake, it's an itsy bitsy microphone.

"Excuse me? Officer Simpson? Officer Watson?"

"Yeah? I'm Officer Simpson, this is Watson. Who are you?"

"Josh Conrad, Channel 7 News. I understand you're heading the Indian Godfather case."

"The what? What are you talking about?"

"Oh. Maybe you haven't seen my reports. The guy's head, the elephant body in the ravine. We're calling it the Indian Godfather case. Well, I'm calling it that on my nightly news reports. No one else is yet, but they will soon. See, it's like in *The Godfather*, you know, the movie, where that guy ends up in bed with the head of his favourite horse, remember? Except in this case it's an East Indian gang, so, *wala*, Indian Godfather."

Simpson stares at Josh Conrad. "Get lost," he says.

Delilah stares at Josh Conrad. "Wanna Timbit?" she asks.

DELILAH

I'm trying to explain to Simpson why I find Josh Conrad attractive. Simpson thinks I have no taste. He says Josh Conrad looks like a large, hard turd. And besides, he says, Josh Conrad is an ambulance-chaser, a newshound, and a television reporter to boot, which is the worst kind. I tell him I've seen Josh Conrad on the news once or twice, even if I didn't recognize him right away when he came up to us. He does this thing called *Action News* where he does all this investigative news gathering. It must be a big deal for Channel 7 to send him out to this one. I think he's cute, I tell Simpson. Don't you? Simpson snorts. Hey Simpson, I say, when he said that thing about East Indian gangs, how come you just led him along? I mean, you even gave him a few "contacts" in the East Indian – South Asian – community who had inside information on those gangs. Simpson, you know, I know, the whole detachment knows there are no South Asian gangs around here. Simpson just smiles. I ask him if it was true what he told Josh, that to introduce himself to members of the Hindu community he should say, "*Saala, kya ha la?*" and does it really mean "How are you, my brother-in-law?" and Simpson starts laughing but nods very emphatically. I swear, he says, that's exactly what it means. And he keeps laughing.

SIDDHI

"You told him *what?*"

"I told him what he wanted to hear."

"You *told* him how to throw around insults in Hindi."

"Sorta."

"Without telling him they were insults."

"Look, Sandip, he's an asshole. He wanted to get a scoop by buddying up to important members of the Hindu community. He wanted to know if saying 'Salaam' was a form of respectful greeting. I just sorta told him I was correcting his pronunciation. I said 'Saala' was an even higher form of greeting, that it quite literally meant calling a man your brother-in-law."

"That's *not* what it means."

"Sure it is. You told me yourself. Literally, you said *Saala* means brother-in-law. I'm not responsible for possible misinterpretations."

"And you say *he's* the asshole."

"C'mon, Sandip. He was trying to pin this elephant caper on South Asian gangs. He's trying to find, create if he has to and he will *have* to, roving gangs of bloodthirsty Indian, Pakistani, East African, Caribbean immigrants. He had it coming. I thought you'd be proud of me."

"Raj Kumar punched him in the face. After returning the brother-in-law greeting."

"Mad at me, Sandip?"

"Nah. Actually, I wish I could've been there."

"Yeah. Me too. That Conrad guy riles me. D's kinda sweet on him, did I tell ya?"

"Yeah, you did. Coupla times."

"Oh."

"Greg?"

"Yeah?"

"C'mere."

SIDDHI

"What're you writing down?"

"Just some ideas for *Action* tomorrow."

"Yeah, like what?"

"Well, I figure if the Indians are going to be so hostile, I'll approach the older white community. Y'know, suss out their fears, anxieties, that sorta thing."

"You mean fearmongering?"

"Listen, we don't make the news, we just report it."

"Yeah. Know what?"

"What?"

"I don't like what you stand for. I don't like what you do."

"Yeah, I know."

"But I'm attracted to you."

"Yeah, I know."

"Why is that, do you think?"

"Dunno. Maybe you secretly respect what I do. It's really a lot like your job, y'know. We're all in this to stop the bad guys and make this a safer place for law-abiding citizens."

"No, that's not it. I think it's that you don't really have a clue, do you? I mean, about how life works, who likes you and who doesn't. Like, that sorta stuff, the sorta stuff that affects normal people, doesn't even faze you, does it?"

"Guess not. Maybe that's why I'm a journalist."

"Maybe that's why you're a jerk."

"That too. Tell me, what is it you first noticed about me?"

"Um. You were colour co-ordinated. You don't see that in men much."

"I was all in black."

"Uh-huh."

"What else."

"Well, it sounds silly."

"Naw, go on, you can tell me."

"No, it's just too, well, you know, silly."

"Please."

"Well, okay. I knew when I first set eyes on you that here was the opportunity for the relationship of a lifetime, completely physical and absolutely unemotional."

"Hm. And why is that?"

"Cuz, Josh, like I said. No way in the world am I ever going to *like* you, let alone feel attached to you."

"Oh. Huh. Yeah. Really?"

"Really. Sorry. Now take off your clothes."

JUDGE McECHERN

"All rise."

Judge McEchern hears this and begins to move his weary body, one limb at a time, but his arms, his legs, are stuck in concrete and he can't seem to move at all.

"Don't get up, Ernie," says the voice.

Very few people call Judge McEchern Ernie. He looks in the direction of the voice but can't see through the dark. He is sightless and paralyzed.

"Open your eyes, Ernie," says the voice.

Judge McEchern opens his eyes. The room is very bright and it takes his eyes a moment to adjust. Then he makes out Harry Hargood sitting in a chair in the corner.

"Hey, Ernie buddy, howya doin'?" says Judge Hargood.

"Okay, I think," says Judge McEchern. "Where am I?"

"Hospital, Ernie buddy. The wife found ya passed out in your den at four in the morning, hand down your shorts and, I'm quoting yer wife, Ernie, swear to god, 'looking like he was trying to unscrew his own plumbing.'"

"Jesus."

"Yeah, well, she got you rushed right into emerg and the doctor, heh heh, the doctor tells me it took two orderlies and a very displeased emergency nurse to unpry ol' Ernie McEchern's fingers from his prized possessions."

"How long have I been here?"

"Death grip, that's what they called it. Said ol' Judge McEchern had a death grip on that place us judges aren't supposed to touch, heh heh."

"Jesus. What day is this? I have court."

"No problem, Ernie. Gotcha covered. Did your morning session and explained everything to the whole crew."

"You *explained* everything? Jesus, Harry, what did you tell them?"

"Told 'em the truth. Told 'em ya hadda be rushed to hospital cuz ya hurt yourself attending to some of your plumbing. Ha."

"Jesus."

"Now, don't you worry 'bout a thing there Ernie. Doctor says you'll be fine in no time. Just be a bit sore when ya walk or sit for the next week or so."

"Harry? When you were in court this morning. . . ."

"Tell me, Ernie buddy. You can tell me. What exactly were ya doing down there?"

"This may sound strange, but in that case, the one with that Indian university prof. . . ."

"I mean, did ya find this in a book or somethin'? Or was it one of them phone lines?"

"Now, I'm not crazy or anything like that, but. . . ."

"Or was this just like a coincidental thing, like you were holding on for Mary's sake and then just forgot to breathe or let go or somethin'?"

"And I know you didn't actually sit the case or anything like that, but before you set it over, I was wondering. . . ."

"Or maybe, this is what I'm thinkin' of, there was someone with you, eh Ernie, someone with you who just got spooked when you fished out like that and left so's you got found by the missus?"

"You didn't happen to notice an elephant in the court, did you?"

"What's that, Ernie?"

"An elephant."

"Sweet Jesus. An elephant?"

"Yeah."

"No, really? You were with an elephant?"

"Yeah, well maybe not a real elephant, but this guy with an elephant's head."

"A *guy*? Jesus."

"Look, Harry, it's just something I saw once. Doesn't mean anything. Forget I ever said anything."

"Sure, Ernie. An elephant. Jeez."

PARVATI

Knock-knock.

If you don't knock he'll never look up. So you do. He looks up. Siva. No doubt about it. Siva from the corner of the lip to the edge of the ear. Siva from the drooping tip of that nose back to the deep-warm cut of that hairline. Siva from the smooth cleft of chin to the dark recesses of throat. Siva.

He stares at you.

You stare at him.

"You Dr. Sribhaiman?" you ask.

"Uh. Oh. Yeah, uh-huh." He's nervous. He recognizes you but he doesn't recognize recognizing you. Yet.

"Parvati." You say this.

He looks startled. "Sam," he says.

You step inside and close the door.

GANESH

When she closes the door, I am embarrassed that I, their son, should be present at their reunion. I would turn around and give them grace of a moment alone, but being made of sandalwood and all, I do the next best thing, which is to divert my attention as a polite gesture. Not that Sam will appreciate this, but Parvati will. She smiles. I look over at Varadharajan's book; its cover is splayed open just enough so that I can peer inside and catch a glimpse of her introduction.

My interest in this traffic of selves and others . . .

"So they call you Sam?"

"Uh, yes, I s'pose they do."

"Or Mr. S?"

"Sometimes."

"Tell me, Sam. Why not *Dr. S?*"

"Um. I'm not sure. Could be cuz I don't like doctors very much."

"Then you don't like yourself?"

"Mebbe. Sometimes."

"Or you don't know yourself?"

. . . colonizers and colonized, men and women, colour and whiteness, is that of a member of the familiar, if still anomalous, breed of intellectual émigrés . . .

"That might be true, Ms. – ?"

"Parvati."

"That's right. You said. Mebbe that's true, Parvati. So tell me. What can I do for ya?"

. . . or, as they are now called, "native informants." My contribution to the vexed enterprise of inscribing the margins . . .

"I needed to talk to someone. I needed to talk to you. It's a matter of – mutual interest, I believe."

"I see. And this mutual interest?"

"It's hard to explain, really. Well, it's hard to explain here." Parvati looks up at me. I continue to read but my presence is all too present for this reunion. She tells me this with a brush of her eyes. I read more intently.

. . . of representing the colonized, and of letting, so to speak, Caliban curse freely, must therefore be accomplished with both . . .

"Here?"

"Yes, here. Not here."

"I'm afraid I don't understand."

"No, of course. I need to explain, of course. But not here. I want to go for some chai."

"Chai?"

"Yes. Chai. Now, please."

. . . difficulty and delicacy.

When they exit the room, Sam leaves the light on. He always leaves the light on if he will be back before long. He has a class to prepare for this afternoon. And a department meeting right after that. Tomorrow morning he has several appointments with graduate students and, because papers are due in a week, there will likely be a number of drop-in appointments during his office hours. Plus, of course, he has to finish and fax off an abstract which was due yesterday but for which he got a gracious two-day extension, the conference just wouldn't be the same without you Sam, just get us something in by Thursday, okay? So Sam leaves the light on.

He does not return for three days.

GANESH

Babiji has been unusually attentive to me the past few days. Every morning she brings fresh flowers and lays them at my feet. For a while she was even buying tins of condensed milk which she would feed me, globs of it, but that proved too thick and syrupy. I would eat as much as I could, but eventually, a crusty residue would cover my lips and trunk and I would look – and feel – like Babiji's grandchildren, playing outside in the snow and coming in with snot all over their faces which Babiji would have to remove with none-too-tender swipes from a damp J-cloth. No, the second time Babiji had to clean off my face she thought the petrified sugar-milk was starting to eat away at my brass finish, *such a bad thing, this will never do* and she used the rest of the condensed milk in her morning tea for a week.

But she still pays me a lot of attention. I still receive twice-daily offerings of milk, and sometimes Babiji sprinkles in some brown sugar before feeding me, and when she does this she giggles cheekily, as if she is performing an illicit task. Maybe she thinks she is fooling the god of elements, feeding me sweetened milk on the sly.

The best part of all this attention, though, is that Babiji talks to me more than she used to. Not that she didn't use to talk to me – *good morning, Ganeshji, how are you today, look outside very sunny very good, today I am not feeling well* – but she talked about little of substance. And I didn't feel that special since she talked to most of the inanimate objects around the house the same way: *you're a baadmash and you know it*, she would curse at the television, her tiny fist balling up as she threatened this character or that on her afternoon shows; *my, but you are very pretty today, you look so fresh, so clean* to cut flowers or the living room window pane or sometimes even to her microwave; *let me up, you baymaan ka bucha, I really must go to the toilet now and you've made me wait too long,* she would say to the couch as she strained to stand.

Babiji was always a talkative sort.

But now she has new energy. She is excited. And, so it appears, it is me who is exciting her. *Saw you on television again last night, ji,* stroking my forehead and removing a bit of grime with her thumb. *You gave that saali blonde girl such a fright she fell right on her chuter, bumpa.* She grins at this and shows me her full set of teeth, which always amazes me at how straight they are, not a spot of orthodontic work, but straight as can be. Then she is serious. *It is good you have come back, Ganeshji, things were getting far too easy for bad people and far too difficult for good people. We need you, ji, for those wonderful things you put in the path and later take away. Yes, this is very good. Here, I will get you some rose water.*

Babiji totters off to fetch some rose water. When she comes back, she is frowning. She dips her right fore and middle fingers in the jar of rose water and starts to sprinkle it about my head.

Those poor people, though, you confuse them terribly. That man and that woman they go looking looking everywhere for your body and for your father and it is all very strange for them. She dips, sprinkles. *That policeman, I think he is very friendly with Sandip. They were very quiet together like they were used to that. I think Sandip needs to be married. What do you think, Ganeshji?* Dip, sprinkle. *Maybe Sandip could become friendly with that policewoman. She seemed very nice. But, no, I think a nice Indian girl would be better, don't you think so? I think so.*

I smell very rosy. Babiji dips her fingers again and touches the wetness to her forehead, then to just above her lip. She smells very nice, too. She reaches into the fold of her sari and pulls something out. She seems to want to hide this from me. Then she picks up the pack of wooden matches near my feet, the matches she uses for lighting sandalwood and jasmine incense. Perhaps she will light some incense for me, but she usually does this in the evening. No, she is fumbling with something in her hand now. It is a package of some sort, triangular, thick. I think I see my face reflected on it. Now I know. Babiji smiles. *Don't tell anyone, ji.* She strikes a match, watches it flare, then brings it to her lips. *Little sins.*

She lights her bidi and slips the Ganesha brand package into the folds of her sari.

This is her new habit, one she picked up from the movies, she tells me. *I want to be more modernized,* she says, *a real modern woman.* None of her friends would ever smoke bidis – too uncouth and smelly. But she saw a woman, an *Indian* woman, sneaking and smoking them on that movie named after spices even though it had nothing to do with spices. *This is how we Indian women should behave in Canada,* she tried telling her friends. *After all, it's in the movies.* But they would not listen to her and they certainly would not smoke those smelly little cigarettes. So she smokes them in private. With me.

ACTION NEWS . . . IN THE RIVER VALLEY

Tempers are flaring in this normally subdued riverside community.

The cause: ethnic gangs.

The result: a town gripped by fear and ripped apart by violence.

Last week a group of fishermen, out for a laidback day on the river, came across a gruesome discovery. Here in the weeds by the shore, they found the detached head of an East Indian man, his eyes frozen open in the terrifying moment of his death. But there was more. Right next to the lifeless head, these fisherman found a headless body—not of a human, but of an elephant.

The mystery: No one has been able—or willing—to identify the victim, nor has there been any sign of his body. As for the elephant re-mains, well, the story just gets curiouser and curiouser, as Alice might say in Wonderland. No elephants in this region, or anywhere for that matter, have been reported missing.

Who is this tragic dead man? Where did this elephant come from? To get some answers, this reporter checked with some of his sources in the local East Indian community. People are so afraid that talking to me would get them in trouble with the gangs that, no sooner had I greeted them they responded with verbal insults, raised voices . . . even fists.

I'm here to tell you that this reporter escaped with only minor scrapes and bruises—but what will happen next time? For these answers and other questions, I remain your man on the scene, Josh Conrad, Action News.

SIDDHI

Delilah and Josh have finished making love. Having finished somewhat earlier than Delilah, Josh had begun to think of tomorrow's *Action* coverage of this Indian Godfather story, which was rapidly going nowhere. As he went through the motions in what he believed to be a practiced and proficient manner, Josh thought of how he might make this story more interesting. A fresh murder, creating some sort of serial-event, would be helpful, but Josh knew this was unlikely to happen. Maybe a protected-source interview with an Indian gang member, Josh thought, the type where the interviewee was backlit or, better still, computer-fuzzed beyond recognition. The trouble was, Josh remembered, the severe lack of Indian gang members, at least ones willing to come forth. Delilah had told him, the Staff Sergeant had told him, all the other media folk had told him that there really weren't any Indian gangs in the area. Still, Josh thought, if he could maybe find some young guy who *wanted* to be part of a gang and maybe wouldn't mind admitting his complicity in the Indian Godfather affair. . . .

"Um, Josh?"

"Huh?"

"You can stop now, thank you."

"Oh. Have you? . . . I mean. . . ."

"It's okay. Thanks anyway."

"Oh . . . Delilah? . . . Are there any, like, Indian youth clubs or anything around here?"

"South Asian."

"What?"

"It's a term thing. South Asian." Delilah lifts herself up on one elbow, watching Josh's arm slide down her waist as she does. He's actually quite good, she tries to convince herself, when he puts his mind to it. She reaches for the remote by the bedside table. She clicks.

"Well, whatever. Anything like that. Where the Indian kids hang out, I mean."

There is a man on a rowing machine. He bulges everywhere. He smiles. His body is an oil slick. Click.

"I've told you, Josh. No marauding South Asian gangs. No gangs, period."

There is a woman chatting happily away on the phone. She, apparently, is the woman of someone's dreams. She smiles. She will talk for $3.99 per minute, Visa or Mastercard. Click.

"I know, you've said. But something's going on. I mean, they beat me up, didn't they? They must've beat me up for a reason."

There is that milk commercial woman, holding a ceramic saucer. She moves toward a short, pudgy statue. She smiles. It looks like the statue starts to move.

"They beat you up because you're stupid. And gullible. *And* Raj Kumar hardly brushed your face."

The statue *is* moving. It's not just moving. It's coming to life. The wooden trunk disengages from its source, becomes flesh and hair, wraps itself around the milk commercial woman and lifts her up.

"It was more than a brush. . . . You know this guy? . . . Besides, I've always bruised quite easily. Corpuscles close to the skin or something like that. . . . What d'ya mean I'm gullible?"

Delilah looks down at her waist. She grasps Josh's wrist, lifts his arm away from her belly, tosses it toward him.

The trunk noses across the screen. A jerky camera keeps it in check. The trunk flails for a jug of milk, tips it over. A jerky camera tracks back to its source, a huge and hairy elephantine head. Below the head, a human body, light brown. A human head. An elephant body. An elephant head. A human body. Delilah reaches across Josh's body to get to the phone. Josh, thinking she is reaching out to caress his face after insulting him, lifts himself to one elbow to meet her gentle hand.

In karate, which Delilah studied in the academy, when delivering a blow one should not focus on the plane of the target but should always imagine going through the target.

In physics, which Delilah studied as part of her science training for veterinary school, one learns that two solid objects may not occupy the same space at the same time.

In cubism, which Delilah has never studied but enjoys nonetheless, one may notice how, in an effort to perceive the world from several positions at once, the artist frequently places features, such as noses, in various positions upon the face.

The crunch of open palm meeting nostril cartilage is a loud crunch. The crunch is one Delilah mentally records as a satisfying crunch. Momentarily, she feels badly that she does not feel badly at having quite possibly broken Josh's nose.

"Sorry," she says, and makes her arm and palm reverse their trajectory slowly so that she imagines she feels cartilage almost-but-not-quite springing back, accordion-like.

"By dose," shrieks Josh.

"Sorry," Delilah reiterates, now re-routing her arm and palm to detour around the image of Josh-holding-nose-with-both-hands to reach for the phone.

"You boke by dose!"

Delilah reaches for the phone. The phone rings. She picks it up.

"Yeah," she says, watching far too calmly as a baby geyser of blood erupts between Josh's fingers. "Hey, Simpson. I was just about to call you."

MR. S

So that's how I met Parvati. We left my office and, I can't hardly describe this, but it felt like we left the planet. I know that sounds looney, but that's how it felt. Like we left the planet dancing. The whole time I was gone I can only remember looking at her like she'd been there forever, like I'd been with her forever. I know this sounds like schlock, don't you think I know that? But you asked, didn't ya?

So it was like that for three days. I mean, it didn't feel like three days, nowhere near it, I mean we didn't sleep, but when I finally got back to the office an' I got in and turned on my computer, that's what it said, that it was three days later.

What'd we do? Well, that's the weird part. Okay, weirdest part. It's like everything she said I already knew and it was like every time I opened my mouth ta speak, she was already hearing it. And when she put fruit in her mouth, I tasted it. That's how weird it was.

Where were we? I guess we were at my place, I dunno. Yeah, it must've been cuz I remember – shit, I remember. Yeah. She – no, it was me – I wanted her to see the shiv. I mean, I had to show this to her, show her this amazing sword that, for god know's what reason, I'd never showed to no one else except for the customs guy when we came back from India. I can't explain it. Looks like I can't explain most of this shit. But, like before, it was like she'd already seen the shiv before I thought of showing it to her, and when I did pull it out of the closet where I kept it, behind some boxes of old clothes I haven't got rid of yet and some student finals from a coupla years back, it was like she just waited there in my room and knew what I was doing. Her and me? Well, I guess. But this is all so weird. Ya gotta believe me. I don't know nuthin about this kid that got killed. The boy is unslain. I've never even been down in that part of the river valley where you said you found the head and part of that elephant. Besides, the elephant, he gave of his head willingly. This just can't be happening. Oh, one more thing, yeah. Her kid. I dunno how he got there. But all of a sudden it was like springtime and we were like in this enormous meadow and it smelled like heather. And I wuz lookin' for Parvati and I called her and then I saw this kid, hers I guess, just standin' between these two rocks. And, like, I could hear somethin', or maybe I could just feel it, but I knew Parvati was behind those rocks and that this kid was in the way. Look, I don't know where all this is coming from. Can I have a glass of water?

DELILAH

Nothing fits. I'm going over and over the tapes of this Sribhaiman professor. He sounds like a wacko. If this were an ordinary slasher case I'd go tell the Crown to wind up the courtroom cuz we have our guy. But something just doesn't fit. Something about his story. What does this part mean: *The boy is unslain.* The boy is unslain? Where'd this guy suddenly come up with an expression like that? Who says "unslain"? Hell, who says "slain"? It's like he knows more than he's gonna say, or more than he can possibly say. Damn, I'm starting to babble like him. And that elephant, that wasn't the biggest elephant in the world, but how the hell does someone take off an elephant's head? So maybe we've only got a photo of that "shiv" Sribhaiman keeps blabbing on about, but a sword's a sword. Whatever took that elephant's head off had gears and pulleys and an effing amount of horsepower behind it. I checked the wound myself. Clean. Dead clean. One swipe clean. I can't think of any*thing* that could do a number like that, let alone anybody. That's why this prof's story doesn't check out. And what about this: *Besides, the elephant, he gave of his head willingly.* Here we go again, Shakespeare 101. Well, maybe, after all, the guy is in classics or Asian studies or whatever. Who can figure?

MR. S

Sex? Yeah, I guess. I mean, yeah, I did, we did. I – with Parvati. I mean I know we did, but I don't really remember, y'see? Look, I'm no psycho, it's just that the particular memory of having sex isn't there, like I don't remember what she did or what I did or how it started or how it stopped. I just remember kinda being in sex, y'know?

Sex. Huh. I guess.

SIMPSON

Sex? Yeah, I guess. I mean, yeah, I did, we did. I – with Sandip. Sure, just before I called you. I mean, not *just* before, but a couple of minutes. 'Dip flipped on the TV, I remember. Said, "Hey Greg, lookit this," cuz I was just dropping off, so I looked up and there was that model, what's her name, Sandy something, with that trunk around her middle and then the camera cuts to the statue, the elephant.

DELILAH

Sex? Yeah, I guess. I mean, yeah, I did, we did. I – with Josh. Well, *he* had sex, if you know what I mean. Then he starts talking about *Action News* and I turned on the TV. I was just flipping around and I stopped on that show, that late-night thing. And I saw the dairy-advertising woman spilling her milk and then the elephant. Or the elephant head. That's what I was thinking: elephant's head, man's body, and here we were looking for an elephant's head and a man's body, and even though it sounded real fantastic, I figured I should call you.

But you called me first.

Just after I broke Josh's nose.

GANESH

When Sam slams the door, the coffee-table book *The Last Empire*, which I can see emblazoned in gold on the spine, begins to slip off the shelf. I use all my telekinetic energy to keep it from falling, because even if it is a colonialist photo-album, I am, after all, lord of written projects and, by extension, of books. So I use all my energy to keep the book from falling.

It falls anyway.

Flies open, pages whirring like they're trying to flap and regain a perch, but avail-less. I see a hundred images flash by. A Maharaja's funeral pyre, portraits of Hindu and Sikh and Marwaree and Tamil and Parsi, a badminton party in Rawalpindi, a quotation from Lord Mountbatten ("India is written across my heart"), the Maharaja of Gwalior who proved his palace ceiling would support the world's largest chandelier by hoisting one of his own largest elephants to the top, dead bears and tigers lying before hunting parties, acrobats, scores of British and loyalist Indian troops, child brides, royal baths, and more and more and more.

Flap flap crunch. A satisfying crunch. The book lands spine down, pages scrunched. The Spivak article, once paper-clipped and inserted between pages 56 and 57, floats down bit by bit, settling gently around the mangled book. *Can* swish swish *the sub* swish swish *altern* swish *speak?* I read the boldfaced title.

Eyes cast down, I can see the two photographs staring up at me.

The first is stark. Two figures, turbaned, occupy the center of the frame. They are hanging by their necks from a single crossbeam. Their hands are tied behind their backs. One man is shirtless, the other wears a kurta. Neither wears shoes. They are being gazed upon by eleven Indian army regulars, some of whom stand at attention with sabres on their shoulders. The caption tells me the photograph was taken by one Felice A. Beato. Felice A. Beato has called this photograph *The Hanging of Two Rebels*, and the editors have subtitled this "the Indian Mutiny, 1858."

The second photograph undoubtedly occurs later in the book, but this page is bent back, torn in the corner, so it appears to rise out of the first photograph. Here I see an aging, balding Muslim man. His face is dead centre of the photograph. A bowl of a hookah, out of focus in the foreground, leads up toward the pipe just below his right eye. He is lying down. It does not appear that he will ever get up. He is *The Last Mughal, Bahadur Shah II, in Exile*, according to photographer P. H. Eagerton. The editor tells me that "Bahadur Shah was exiled to Rangoon for his part in the uprising of 1857, in which he sided with the mutineers. A poet of distinction, his life in exile was a popular subject of curiosity for British tourists to post-Mutiny Delhi."

Because Sam has left the lights on, because I do not know when he will return, I study these photographs. And I read the twelve pages of Spivak's article that have landed both face-up and within my line of vision.

I do this for three days.

VIGHNESVARA

Placing obstacles. Removing obstacles. Placing removing placing removing placing removing. What a job. It's not the activity that makes this work so intense, it's the subtlety. Now, *anyone* can lay down an obstacle, and just about anyone can take it away. The subtlety is the way in which the obstacle is placed, the thought that goes into determining exactly what a given subject will likely need to do to get around the obstacle. That's the craft. That's the art.

I am in the interrogation room with Simpson and Mr. S. They have been at it for several hours now. Occasionally Simpson takes a break and Delilah moves in. Mr. S does not get to take a break. When Simpson and Delilah meet outside the interrogation room in their tagteam game, they talk about trying to wear Mr. S down. Simpson thinks Mr. S is holding something back, something that will likely incriminate him. Delilah also thinks Mr. S is holding something back, but she's more unsure about his guilt. Because Simpson and Delilah are also tired, they snarl a bit at each other's fallibilities.

But they are both right.

Sometimes I drift across the interrogation room to the large mirror and I float through the mirror to the other side. I know this is not the conventional way of using this device, but mirrors have never been much of an obstacle for me. Simpson and Delilah make use of the two-way mirror in a more conservative manner. Mr. S knows it's a two-way mirror, not just because he's seen mirrors like this on television, but because the lights in the observation room are too bright, the lights in the interrogation are rather dim, and the mylar used to make the mirror two-way isn't the real expensive stuff so Mr. S can occasionally see a bit of movement in the observation room. He can also make out a spot of red in the top right corner which indicates to him he is being videotaped. Occasionally Mr. S thinks he should call a lawyer, but I convince him that such an obstacle would not be worthwhile. Mr. S, because he is tired, believes the voice telling him not to call a lawyer is his subconscious.

But this process is becoming tedious. What's needed is a good obstacle. I drift into the observation room to observe. I stand beside Delilah and we both listen to Simpson and Mr. S's voice through the speaker.

"Want something to drink?" asks Simpson. "More coffee, juice maybe?"

Mr. S is about to say juice would be fine, but then a little voice inside his head changes his mind.

"Could I have some milk?"

"Milk?"

"Yeah, milk. Do you have a milk machine around here?"

"Yeah. Sure. Just a moment."

Simpson goes out the door of the interrogation room and Delilah and me go out the door of the observation room. We all meet in the hall. We all walk down the corridor together to the milk machine.

"He's not budging," says Simpson.

"Maybe he doesn't know which way to budge," suggests Delilah.

"Why does he just sit there making up stories? If I were in his place I'd have called a lawyer by now."

They are at the milk machine. Simpson fishes for quarters in his pocket. He comes up with three, Delilah hands him one.

"Maybe," says Delilah, "he's waiting to tell us something."

"Yeah, like what?" Simpson drops the quarters in, punches all the buttons at once, and bends down to pull the milk from the chute.

"I dunno. Something special."

We all go back to our respective rooms, Simpson with a cool milk in his hand. We settle back into our places. Simpson hands Mr. S the milk. Delilah and me peer through the two-way mirror. Something like a heatwave is making things look funny, thinks Delilah. Just a minor obstacle, really. Inside the interrogation room, Mr. S tears open his carton of milk and takes a big gulp. He is face to face with Simpson. As Mr. S drinks, Simpson appears to slip. He begins to fall backward. Mr. S reaches out for him with his free hand and then tries to slow Simpson's fall by grabbing his shoulder. Simpson is heavy and keeps falling. Mr. S reaches out with another hand and grabs the other shoulder. Simpson is halfway to the ground now and gravity is doing its work. Mr. S reaches out with another hand and places it under the small of Simpson's back. Simpson is almost touching the ground now. His head is beginning to lash back. It will hit the cement floor. Delilah gasps. I don't worry. Mr. S reaches around with another hand and places it behind Simpson's head, then with another hand and cradles Simpson's neck. Simpson touches down delicate as a feather, arms and arms and arms of Mr. S making for a soft landing. As Simpson reaches his horizontal position he looks up to see Mr. S taking another swig of milk with his free hand.

Simpson says thank you and gets up. Mr. S nods and finishes his milk. Simpson rushes out of the interrogation room and into the observation room. Delilah is already fumbling with the video camera.

"What the hell happened in there?" bellows Simpson. Delilah has the tape out. "Let's see," she says calmly although she is anything but calm.

They leave the observation room to go across the hall where the detachment sometimes shows training videos and sometimes shows other types of videos, mostly seized ones. Delilah plops the tape into one of the machines.

"D, did you see what happened? Am I just imagining –"

"I saw," says Delilah, cuing the tape. "I just wanna see it again."

On the monitor, Mr. S is sitting alone. The door opens and Simpson walks in carrying a carton of milk. He gives this to Mr. S. Mr. S gets to his feet to greet Simpson and to receive his milk. He tears the carton open. There is a brief blip on the monitor. Simpson turns to face Mr. S and, for no apparent reason, begins falling backward. Mr. S reaches out with his free hand and catches Simpson by the shoulder. There is another blip. The videotape shows Simpson hurtling backward and Mr. S sipping his milk with one hand and the other hand on Simpson's shoulder. Simpson's fall begins to slow, then stop. Mr. S appears to be holding Simpson horizontally with only one hand on his shoulder. This is a good trick, but this is no trick.

"What went on in there?" whispers Simpson.

"Like I said," says Delilah, "maybe he was waiting for something special to say."

GANESH

I have lied. That was for effect. I do not stare at the same two photographs and twelve pages of Spivak for three whole days. I stare at this spectacle for the entire rest of the day after Sam leaves, through the night, and the rest of the next day until 10:34 p.m. I know it is 10:34 p.m. because when the door opens and Durga walks in she is talking to her husband on a cell-phone. "Hahn, ji," she says, coddling the phone between cheek and shoulder as she wiggles the keys free from the door, "it is just twenty-five minutes to eleven. Nahin, one minute earlier than that." And so I know.

"Teek-hahn, I must go now. I will see you in the morning. Hahn, I will call at three. Ji, goodbye."

Durga flicks the cell phone closed with her left hand and automatically goes to switch the lights on with her right. She brushes past the switch before realizing the lights are already on. Aara, such wastage, she thinks. And even though she hardly sees any of the professors at the university who almost always leave before five unless they have a night class, Durga is surprised at this because she believes Dr. Sribhaiman, whom she knows only as S. Sribhaiman from the nameplate on his door, is a frugal and caring person. She has never met Sam, but she imagines him to be in his early sixties, just a few years older than her, and very well-mannered. She also imagines that were Dr. Sribhaiman ever to see her in the halls or, god forbid, anywhere in public, he would pretend not to notice her, or, if he did notice her, it would be as a tourist looks at friezes of Durga on pillars at Mamallapuram, with curiosity. Despite these thoughts,

Durga does not think ill of Dr. Sribhaiman. He is what he is, she thinks.

She pushes her cleaning trolley into the office and puts the cell-phone in her pocket. She still finds it humorous that she carries such a ridiculous extravagance around with her at night. But that was the concession the big boys made after those three women were attacked, all within two months, just cleaning in this building and the one next door where all the big boys worked. Of course, they did nothing after the first two women were attacked except post security alerts on a few bulletin boards and try their best to downplay the "incidents" in the media. But when that third woman was attacked and the union met and got very angry about the whole lack of concern and threatened not only to strike but to ask for an external investigation, well, that frightened the big boys. What Durga found most humorous about this was that the big boys decreed that all the cleaners should carry cell-phones, but the only place they could get cell-phones, what with all these budget cuts although it didn't seem to Durga that any of the big boys were going hungry, was from within their own ranks. They were the only ones to have cell-phones paid for by the university, surprise surprise. So now, every time she and the others checked in, they were given a cell-phone for their shift "to be used only in the case of emergency or pre-assigned contact." Those were the words on their new contract. She and the others were unclear on what "pre-assigned contact" really meant or how that would help them from getting attacked sometime during the night, but they were told they could check in with their husbands or wives or children twice per night and the university would pay for that. This would create what the president called "an atmosphere of peace of mind for the families of these hard-working caretakers." That's what he said to the television reporter who showed up at his office, dressed all in black and shoving that microphone everywhere around the president's face. Durga and two others were on a break watching television when they saw that, and they howled.

I know all this because Durga spends a lot of time in Sam's office talking to me. And because she always likes to "do a thorough job," she works at cleaning this or that the whole time she is talking to me so that Sam's office is the neatest, shiniest, most dust-free office in the building, I am sure. Sometimes she even brings in a smidgen of sandalwood oil to freshen me up.

Durga is in the office and she sees the mess on the floor. She shakes her head sadly and looks up at me, as if it was my fault. I telepathically tell her that I was trying to *stop* this disaster, but she doesn't notice. She stoops down and begins by picking up the Spivak article, one page at a time. She collects it into a neat unordered heap and places it on the corner of Sam's desk. Then she picks up the book and shakes it off. She sets it down on the side of Sam's table and begins idly flipping through pages. I cannot see what she is looking at because she stands between me and the book. She flips through the book for one or two minutes. Then she sighs and takes out her spray bottle. Today she is not doing floors and in most offices will only empty waste baskets. But, in Sam's office, perhaps because she thinks she might like Sam or because she thinks the office should stay clean because of me, she will wipe off the bookshelves and clean the door handle. As she does this I look at the place where the book is now open. This is in the middle of the book. Again, there are two photographs, but now the pages are not scrunched.

The first photograph is called *Englishman with His Dog and Horse*. A moustachioed man in a bowler hat is seated, his right arm around the neck of a beagle, his left grasping the handle of an umbrella which rests between his legs. Behind him is a saddled mare posing for the picture. To the right of the horse, holding her head, is a turbaned, barefoot, dark-skinned man, the groom no doubt. He looks at the horse. She looks at him. I look at the caption again. An Englishman, his dog, his horse.

The second photograph is called *Englishman Being Served Coffee in Bed*. Just left of centre stands an Indian woman whose dark face seems all the more dark owing to the white-white frock and headcovering she wears. In her hand, the only other bit of skin showing, is a huge white coffee cup. The room is in total disarray. There are boots and shoes and empty bottles and half-filled glasses everywhere. On the floor is a riding crop. On the wall, a rack of guns, some pictures of what appears to be Queen Victoria, and a pair of skulls that look bovine or ungulate in origin. To the right and below the woman, laying atop a fringed flannel blanket, his left arm curled behind his head and his right drifting off the side of the bed is, presumably, the Englishman in bed to whom coffee is being served.

"Ucha. That's enough for today," says Durga, performing one last squirt in the general direction of the desk and wiping off the droplets from the chipped finish. "Goodbye, Ganeshji."

As she starts to swing the door shut, I focus again on the two photographs. There are a few droplets of cleaning fluid on the Englishman in bed.

The lights go out.

SIDDHI

"What'd she ask you, that time?"

"Who?"

"Mrs. Thakkar. Before she told you about the elephant god coming back to life, I mean. She asked you a couple of questions."

"She did?"

"She did. And you remember, don't you? You're just not saying."

"Oh, that. That was just family stuff. How are your uncles, aunts, that sorta thing."

"Oh, really. Then how come you avoided her questions?"

"I didn't avoid them. We had other business to attend to so I just brought her back to the photograph."

"You avoided her questions. Just like you're avoiding mine. I can always tell when you're avoiding questions, too. Always have."

"Whatcha mean?"

"You purse your lips. And your one eyebrow, that one, raises a bit and starts to quiver. That's how I know. And that's what you're doing right now, see?"

"Okay, I'll tell ya. Babiji was asking about you."

"Me? What? Why?"

"She wanted to know if you were a nice boy. If I was happy with you."

"She what? She knows?"

"And she wanted to know some more personal details. Was your butt as tight and round as Vishnu's, she asked, and was your lingam as heavenly as Shiva's?"

"Bullshit."

"Yah, bullshit."

"So what did she ask?"

"She wanted to know if I was married. She wanted to know if your partner was my girlfriend."

"So whatcha tell her?"

"Christ, Greg, you were *there*. As you so delicately pointed out, I *didn't* answer her. I avoided the questions, remember?"

"Oh, yeah."

"And speaking of avoiding, your parents. When do I get to meet them?"

GANAPATI

And so, Your Honour, what began quite clearly as a case of mistaken, or perhaps untaken, identity, quickly escalated to what the court might consider murder in the first degree. However, I do believe this case takes a turn for the defence, being that it's not just unusual but without precedent, that the alleged victim of the alleged homicide takes the stand on the side of the defence. That is, me.

You have heard me introduced to this court as Vighnesvara, lord of obstacles; Siddhi, manifestation of desire; and, amidst a host of other monikers, the most popular of all, Ganesha, that quaint squat elephant-headed boy who rides a rat and gets to be lord of propitious beginnings and god of written projects and a bevy of other endeavours. But I stand before you in my manifestation of Ganapati, lord of wisdom. Now, I'm the first to admit that this does not mean, by a long shot, that I speak the uninterrupted truth. That would be incredibly dull, particularly so when part of me has this thing about obstacles and, though it might be argued that truth is the most oppressive of obstacles, I prefer to think of the, well, fluidity of stories, the happy merging of fictive and lived realities. All of this notwithstanding, Your Honour, I am the god of wisdom. I'm smart. I know things. I know some things. And what I'm telling you today, before this illustrious court, is that the rumours of my death have been greatly exaggerated. And I say this, not because I've always wanted to say this, but because it is, to the best of my knowledge as Ganapati, lord of wisdom, the truth, or at least a very believable story, or at the very least the best story I can think of at this moment.

Thank you for your indulgence.

JUDGE McECHERN

Judge McEchern looks around his courtroom. They are still laughing at him, all of them, the court clerk, the Crown Prosecutor, the legal aid lawyer , everyone in the gallery. They are laughing at him, he is sure of this.

And why shouldn't they?

Judge McEchern returned to court six weeks ago after a two-day absence for medical reasons. He is sure Harry Hargood did not tell anyone specifically why Judge McEchern was in hospital, but Harry has a way of telling people the truth, the whole truth, and nothing but the truth in very unspecific ways.

Harry Hargood is a gossip.

Judge McEchern is embarrassed.

Every morning for the past six weeks now, Judge McEchern has entered his courtroom from his chambers and stepped quietly up the three steps to his judge table. He does not look at anyone because he is afraid they will either be looking at him in that way or they will be looking at him down there, seeking out even the tiniest sliver of evidence that will prove Harry Hargood a reliable source and Judge McEchern an aging pervert.

So Judge McEchern makes his way as quickly as possible, without making it appear as if he is making his way as quickly as possible, from the door of his chambers to the safe space behind his judge table where the court can only see him from the chest up.

Although he knows this is a paranoid fear, he is afraid someone will bring a pair of those x-ray glasses into the courtroom, just to see if they can see anything unusual which will confirm Judge McEchern's despicable pervert status. Judge McEchern knows this is a paranoid fantasy, partly because he is sure no one in his court would stoop so low, and partly because he knows that those x-ray glasses are a fraud. He has tried them himself and he knows they don't work. Oh, they make people look funny and all, but they don't allow the wearer to actually see through people's bodies or under their clothes like they're supposed to. Someone should take those x-ray glasses manufacturers to court, Judge McEchern thinks, for false advertising.

Judge McEchern tries to rid himself of these consuming thoughts and to concentrate on the proceedings. He is presiding over a homicide case. The accused has elected to be tried by judge alone, something which Judge McEchern both likes and dislikes.

He likes this because it gives him absolute power over everybody in the courtroom because he is the ultimate voice of authority. Already Judge McEchern has laid three charges of contempt: one because an expert witness for the Crown was chewing gum and would not expectorate the offending object and stick it on her nose as she was duly instructed by the court; one because some television guy dressed in black sneezed so violently everyone turned around to look at him and he smiled because this was obviously an intentional disruption; and one because no one had provided a Tamil translator for the court, although that charge was dismissed because Judge McEchern would be no more specific than charging "whoever was responsible" with contempt and since no one claimed liability, the charge was dropped. Come to think of it, thinks Judge McEchern, the Crown stayed proceedings on both his other contempt charges, but that mattered little. Judge McEchern was keeping track of the number of contempt charges he laid, not the number of convictions resulting. That wasn't his job.

He doesn't like this, being sole arbiter of a homicide case without benefit of a jury, because homicide cases tend to be rather long and, as the one-person verdict-deciding body, Judge McEchern has to pay close attention to most of the evidence and testimony. This is particularly difficult because both the accused and the victim are foreigners and a lot of the witnesses have foreign names which make them all the more difficult to keep track of, thinks Judge McEchern. The bottom line is this: one foreigner, whose name Judge McEchern always mispronounces when not altogether forgetting it, has killed another foreigner, whose name no one seems to know but which, if they did know, Judge McEchern would always mispronounce when not altogether forgetting it. These foreigners should all – Judge McEchern pauses, then self-censors his thoughts because of a sudden paranoid fantasy that someone has developed a pair of thought-ray glasses and that they actually work and that someone is wearing them in his courtroom and reading Judge McEchern's mind. Foreigners are nice people, he thinks loudly, articulating each word as he visualizes it on his mental screen. Very nice people.

The only good thing that has occurred over the past six weeks is actually a non-occurrence, thinks Judge McEchern.

To date, during the entire trial, there has been neither hide nor hair of an elephant trace in his courtroom.

VIGHNESVARA

Evidence is a funny thing. You need it to get a conviction in a court of Queen's Bench. But you also need it to get an acquittal in a court of Queen's Bench. Without evidence you can get neither a conviction nor an acquittal in a court of Queen's Bench. Couldn't have thought of a better working obstacle myself. Of course, the Crown Prosecutor, whom I visit regularly in her very busy office, so busy that she never acknowledges my presence, says that this is a moot point. Technically true, she says to her associates, but moot. Moot because a case is never brought to trial without evidence. That is clear. What is not clear, even and maybe especially to herself, is why she is proceeding on this murder case quite to the contrary of her position. She thinks she has made a mistake. But not really. She was only listening to me and now it's up to me to get her, and all the others, out of this in some manner.

I am in the Rocky Mountains. I am looking for evidence. I do not know what kind of evidence, but I know I am looking for some and this should be enough.

I am at a mountain conference centre. Most of the people here are very businessy and they run from room to room listening to people talk about businessy things. Occasionally, when they run from a conference room back to their own bedroom, for which their corporation pays too much money and in which they keep a bottle of scotch by the bedside reading lamp, they will pause to take a deep breath and look up at the mountains. Pretty mountains, they will think to themselves. Very pretty. They may or may not participate in the conference-sponsored nature hike on Saturday, which will

ONCE UPON AN ELEPHANT

take them up an asphalt and stone-stepped route into a canyon and back out again, ending at a giftshop where they can buy plastic figurines of Mounties and souvenir maple sugar, both of which are made over two thousand miles away from these mountains. And if they do participate in such a nature hike, they will stop and smell the fresh air and say to themselves they must get out to the mountains more often.

It is one such gentleman I am following, rushing as he is from what he considers to be a politically important but otherwise very dull bar-graph presentation back to his room where he can have just one sip of scotch before meeting his friends for a drink. He stops to take a deep breath. He looks up. In the bushes near his residence he sees a bushy tail. The bushy tail sees him. Or, rather, the head attached to the body attached to this bushy tail notices the guest.

"Hello," says bushy tail.

"Shoo dog," says the guest.

"I'm not Dog," says bushy tail. "I'm Coyote."

"People shouldn't let their 'dogs run around like that," says the guest, not to Coyote but to himself. "There are wild animals around that could eat a dog like that."

"I am a wild animal. I am Coyote," says Coyote.

But the guest just makes hissing noises and shuffles past Coyote in search of his room, a glass, and a tiny bit of scotch.

I am intrigued with this Coyote. I decide to introduce myself.

"Hello, Coyote," I say.

"Hello, you," says Coyote back, a bit more interested in what he has discovered near the bushes than in me.

"My name is Vighnesvara," I say.

"I see," says Coyote, looking up to look at me for the first time. "Say, you're not from around here, are you?"

"No," I say. "I'm Indian."

"Not like any Indian I ever saw," says Coyote.

"Not that kind of Indian," I say. "I'm from India."

"Is that why you're called Indians?" asks Coyote.

"Exactly," I say.

"The people around here are called Indians, too," says Coyote, "for entirely different reasons."

"What sort of reasons?" I ask.

"Don't ask," says Coyote. "Takes too long."

"I have time," I say.

"Five hundred years?" asks Coyote.

"Okay," I say. "Want me to write this down?" I realize I have no pen with me, something that happens rather regularly I regret to say, what with being lord of written projects and everything, so I reach for my only tusk and start yanking at it.

"I was only joking," says Coyote. "Leave your teeth alone."

"Oh," I say.

"So, Vighnesvera, what brings you up into the mountains?"

"I'm looking for evidence," I say.

"Oh," says Coyote. "What kind of evidence?"

"I don't know," I admit.

"The best kind," Coyote says.

"It's for a murder investigation," I inform him.

"Murder? Whose?" he asks.

"Mine," I say.

"Are you dead?" he asks.

"No, of course not, are you?" I retort.

"Don't get testy," says Coyote. "I was only asking. Besides, you did say you were a murder victim."

"So?"

"So, most murder victims are dead."

"True," I admit. "But I'm not. The Crown is trying to prove this man, well, my father sort of except not really, killed me by cutting off my head."

"Did he?" asks Coyote with a hint of excitement, licking his lips ever so slightly.

"Did he what?" I ask. I am a bit irritated. This Coyote interrupts stories a lot, I think.

"Did he kill you by cutting off your head?"

"I told you," I tell Coyote, "I'm not dead."

"Oh." Coyote's interest fades.

"But he did cut off my head."

"Oh," and, lip-licking, he is interested in my story again.

"So the Crown thinks there's been a murder and I want to prove, I think, that there's been no murder."

"Just a beheading?"

"Yes, except beheadings are usually seen as murder because that's what usually happens when you behead someone."

"I've never beheaded anyone," says Coyote defensively.

"What?"

"You said, 'that's what usually happens when you behead someone,' and I said I've never beheaded anyone."

"It's just a manner of speaking, an expression," I say, "a figure of speech."

"Well, then, watch your figures, please," says Coyote. "They can hurt."

"I'm sorry," I say. "So that's my predicament."

Coyote thinks on this for a long moment. He paws at the ground a bit. He sniffs the air. Then he speaks.

"Why don't you testify?"

"Me, testify?"

"Yeah, you, testify. Someone's said your father is a murderer, right? And that same someone said he, your father, killed you. But you're not dead, right? Just tell that someone you're alive and it'll all be over."

"That might work, Coyote," I say. "You've helped me with my obstacle."

"You're welcome," says Coyote. "I have a question."

"What's that?"

"Who is Crown?"

"Crown?"

"Yeah, Crown. You say this Crown is trying to prove your father killed you. Who is Crown?"

"Oh, the Crown," I say. "The Crown is the name given to the prosecution. It's a metonym, really."

"I see," says Coyote.

"A metonym," I say, anticipating his question, "is when you substitute the part for its whole."

"I never substitute the part for its whole," says Coyote petulantly. "That would never be enough."

"Sorry, my fault," I say. "A metonym is when *someone* substitutes the part for its whole. In this case, the Crown is metonymous for the Queen."

"The Queen?"

"The Queen of England."

"I see," says Coyote. "So the Queen is angry at your father?"

"Well, in a way," I admit.

"And she, the *Crown*, which sits on top of the Queen's head, is ticked off at your father because he, apparently, took off *your* head. Is that right?"

"Metonymously speaking, yes."

"Does this have anything to do with your head?" Coyote asks, eyeing me closely. "I couldn't help noticing that you have an odd-shaped head."

"It's an elephant's," I say proudly. "My father gave it to me."

"I see," says Coyote, nodding as if he gets it all now.

"I have one more question, Vighnesvara."

"Fire away," I say, quite excited at the prospect of testifying in court.

"Do all Indians, your Indians I mean, have these strange courts with Crowns and queens?"

"No, no," I say. "The Crown, the Queen, these are all legacies of the British monarchy, British common law."

"The British," says Coyote, "those are the white ones who came here a while back, aren't they?"

I shrug. "I guess so, I dunno," I say.

"I see," says Coyote. "Know what, Vighnesvara? This is all starting to make sense."

SIDDHI

"Delilah knows about us."

"Saints alive, how did that happen?"

"Dunno, she figured it out."

"Gosh, that woman must be some sleuth. Somehow, through her powers of observation, she has found out who her partner of two years has been sleeping with for these past two years."

"Okay, okay. Got it. But this could be serious, 'Dip. The first step on that slippery slope and all that. If the guys find out —"

"So, what, she's gonna tell 'em?"

"No, of course not, it's just that this is the way these things start. If she knows, how long will it be before someone else figures this out?"

"Hmm. See whatcha mean. This could even get back to your parents."

"Sandip!"

"Speaking of which. . . ."

GANESH

The Sam who returns to his office three days later is not the same Sam who left.

No, that's not quite right.

It's the same Sam. All too much the same Sam. But in between, in that three-day period of whatever, Sam was not-Sam. This I know.

Hello, Sam, I telepathize as he enters his office. He looks deep in thought. He stares at his desk. He flicks on his computer. The only discernible difference for him, I know, would be that the Spivak article, pages out of order, is neatly stacked on the corner of the desk and *The Last Empire* is open and on his desk, not stuffed into the shelf off to my right.

"What the hell has happened?" says Sam.

Well, a lot, I telepathize back. You've been gone for three days. A lot can happen in three days. I tell him about the incident whereby his slamming of the door caused the book to fall and become damaged, how I studied the photographs and various pages of the Spivak article that lay on the floor below me, how Durga, whom he has never met of course, came in and picked up the book and put Spivak back together, how Durga cleaned off the corner of his desk and his door handle and unintentionally, I think, left a few droplets on *An Englishman Being Served Coffee*, which have since dried and blotted so the Englishman looks not only asleep and a messy housekeeper but a bit mottled to boot, how the phone's been ringing at least once an hour during the day ever since he left, even in the evening occasionally, and how his answering machine is likely full of inquisitive to frantic messages from students and colleagues alike, how Durga returned just last night, this time to do the floors, and how she told me about the boy's head that had been discovered in the river valley and what is this world coming to and her husband wants her to call him every hour now because this boy, after all, was an Indian boy and maybe someone has it in for the Indian community. That's what's happened, Sam.

"What the hell has happened to me?" Sam asks again.

Oh, I get it now. The question, rhetorical, and narcissistic on top of that.

"Parvati. Where's Parvati? And her son. My god, what about her son?"

Then something odd happens to Sam. He shuffles things around on his table. He hits the play button on his answering machine and begins jotting down reminders to himself of who he should phone back and in what order. As he listens to the messages with one ear, he picks up the phone and calls seven-six-two-nine, the main office, puts the receiver to his other ear, holding it in place with his shoulder, continues to jot down notes "Nancy," he says into the receiver, "yes, I know . . . yes, of course . . . but . . . but . . . there was an accident, Nancy, I had to be gone, it was all so sudden couldn't tell anyone, but I'm back now . . . yes . . . yes . . . thanks, Nancy, please tell people. I'm back."

Sam hangs up the phone. I can see him forgetting the past three days. At first his eyes show flickers of memory and there's a dance in his heart. I can see all these things. But this is the development of a photographic image in reverse. These things fade and Sam's shoulders sink lower.

He has been gone for three days. When he walked back into his office, he was still connected to that recent past, to Parvati and whatever might have happened with her.

Now he has forgotten. Almost everything.

VIGHNESVARA

Testify. All I have to do is testify. Coyote is right. Smart cookie, that one. Seems almost too easy. Okay, so I testify. No problem getting myself called to the stand. Just have to figure out whether to get called by the defence or the Crown. Defence, I think. More dramatic, a last-minute witness who can undeniably disprove the Crown's airtight case. Yeah, that's it.

Except.

Except in what form do I appear? Ah, there's the obstacle. Me, Vighnesvara, folks tend to ignore, more or less like they're looking right through with x-ray glasses or something. Coyote sees me. But Coyote's not the court. Coyote's not the Crown.

Siddhi? Interesting thought. Have desire flooding the courtroom, a massive free-for-all during which I, Siddhi, explain to the judge, in achy love-etched tones, of course, how I'm sincerely not dead. Love is still alive. That would be a feat.

Ganesh, of course, him, me, too. Maybe a chorus of Ganeshes, a fleet, a covey, a whole gaggle of Ganeshjis, Ganesh-me's. Wooden, brass, plastic, paper, stone, two-dimensional, three-dimensional, sculpted, drawn, bas-relief, video-imaged, holographic, every conceivable representation of Ganesh from temples all over south Asia through the bedrooms and boudoirs of the Americas, yes, all packed onto the witness stand.

"I can't be dead," a million images of Ganesh will sing, "because we're here. We're here, we're elephant-headed, get used to it."

Or, more reasonably and sage-like, Ganapati. My wiser half. Explaining away the improbability of any murder ever taking place in any context past present future. Hmm. Yeah. Ganapati. Ganapati, the Buddhi one, Lord of Wisdom. That'll do.

Time to remove some obstacles.

DELILAH

Josh is watching television. He is watching my television. He is watching himself on my television. Unfortunately, this is not a live broadcast, because then he wouldn't be here, on my bed, watching my television, obviously in love with the images of himself that dance across the screen.

Josh is a jerk.

"Hey Dlylah," he calls out from the bed. He always forgest the second syllable of my name. At first, I thought this was cute. For about thirty minutes I thought this was cute.

Josh is a disgusting human being.

I wander over to the bed. He is grinning. He looks like a raccoon grinning. This is because both his eyes have turned an incredible mural of blue, dark brown, and black. The only thing that makes him look less raccoon-like and, because of this, much less cute, is the plastic nose-splint and pasty bandages across the middle of his face. At first Josh was angry that I had broken his nose. Not for the usual reasons a sentient being would be angry that his nose was broken, that it hurt, that it might have been intentional, nothing like that. Josh was upset because of the way it made him look, the way he would look for the next four weeks. At least. Josh had gone to the best plastic surgeon he could find to ensure he would not have a permanent list to his nose. He was told he would look fine. Whoever had done such a clean break on his nose deserved a medal, the surgeon told him. Josh did not give me a medal. Josh was upset that he would not be able to do his job for the next month or so. He was even more upset that his producer had suggested that he could continue to cover the case but just refrain from doing any standups. He could still be a reporter, a good reporter, his boss told him. He just wouldn't be able to do the summary standup at the end of the piece. That could be handled by the desk, he was told. Josh was outraged. He did not believe in research, he squalled. He did not believe in doing all the work for none of the glory. The truth was, of course, that Josh just liked to see himself on the TV screen. This is why he is now apparently so happy, because he is watching reruns of himself doing standups for Channel 7.

I do not know many people who enjoy watching reruns. Over and over and over again.

I do not know anyone who enjoys watching reruns of old news shows.

Or I did not know anyone like that until now.

"Look't dis," says Josh. "I jusd figgiwwed someding out."

I look at the screen. There is Josh, pre-nosebreak, bleating out some routine end to a story.

"Dey're all de same," says Josh.

He is not disturbed by this. Rather, he is quite elated.

"Don't you see. I say de same ding, or pwetty much, at de end of each repowt. All we have ta do is a bit of caweful ediding, take out de specifics and whatnot, and dis'll pass as Josh Conrad, ond his feet, on de job, and most impowdandly, on camewa!"

I do not say I am delighted. Apparently, Josh expects this of me.

I stare at him unbelievingly. He mistakes this for something else. He reaches out to grab my hand, pulls me on top of him. Maybe one last time, I think. After all, it was pretty good, on and off, until the nose incident. After that the sex

was quite dismal. Not that I could figure out what his nose
had to do with anything.

We make out for a couple of minutes. This is harder than
it sounds when half of the make-out couple has an overly-
sensitive face. Making out basically involves no kissing and a
lot of touching. We start to undress each other. I pull Josh's
black t-shirt over his head, carefully, so as not to re-injure his
nose. He slides his hand down my back, under my jeans. One
last time, I figure. And it better be worth it. We undress each
other quickly, almost as if there is some desire left in both of
us. I look over to see if we have any condoms by the bedside.
Best to get things all packaged up from the start, I figure.
There aren't any there. Josh, surprisingly aware when it
comes to matters that should concern him, like condoms,
follows my gaze.

"I'll be back in a sec," he says, and hefts himself up to
leap over me on the way to the bathroom.

At this moment, or maybe even a moment before, the
phone rings.

The telephone is on Josh's side of the bed. Josh is trying
to clamber over me to get to the bathroom. He is in mid-air,
pushing himself off and over me with one hand, so he
appears to be performing a gymnastics manoeuvre.

A ringing telephone has always caused an instinctual,
almost Pavlovian, response in me. I don't just go for the
phone; I really go for the phone. Doesn't matter what I'm
doing or what's happening – I could be in the shower, sleeping off a twenty-four-hour overtime shift, hanging out talking to the neighbour three doors down – if the phone rings,
I will try to get to it. Okay, sometimes, when I'm really
depressed, I let the phone ring. But even then, not before
that initial, uncontrollable, entirely unintentional response.

I have a great deal of upper body strength. A lot of the guys at work are hard on women, figuring we can't do this or that part of the job, and one of the big criticisms is upper body strength. Women don't have it, they would say. So one night, after three beers at 10-4, I said to one of the guys, I said, "Cam, you and me, right now," and I plopped my elbow down on the table, forearm vertical, international sign of the arm-wrestle challenge. Cam laughed at first, but then he figured he'd lose too much face with the guys if he rejected my challenge and I could see him figuring out how to explain to the guys why he had to do it, arm-wrestle a woman, but that he took it easy on me so as not to hurt me. And so he grinned and plopped his forearm down, and we locked wrists, and the boys gathered 'round, and someone, Kowalski I think, put his hands on our hands and then let go and said, "Go," and we went. Cam started out like a lot of guys start out, just trying to keep his arm stiff so as not to end the fun too early, and so there we were, our arms up and down, both of us smiling, neither of us trying. So about twenty seconds into it, "Ready," I said, and Cam just sorta laughed, and I said, "'kay," and I drove the bastard's wrist so hard into the table there's little knuckle imprints in the red terry-towel tablecloth. "I have a great deal of upper body strength," I said to no one in particular, and leave it at that so neither me nor anybody says, "for a woman."

This is all flashing through my mind as I reach up for the phone, fast, firm, with purpose.

As Josh begins to ascend over my body I notice that he is quite, although not completely, sexually aroused. A week ago I might have been moderately flattered, but that was before I saw that bulge in his shorts one night when he was watching reruns of his own newscasts. Now I am just moderately concerned because my mind is working faster than my fist – and my hand is without good reason clenched into a fist – which is hurtling to answer the phone even though I know it's probably just some carpet sales canvasser.

There is a particular sound that is somewhere between a squish and a thwack, the sort of sound made when you drop a *slightly* overripe vegetable, like an eggplant, onto the floor from a considerable distance. It is not an altogether unpleasant sound, but it's a distinctive sound of loss, a sound which makes you say, "Oh look, now I've gone and dropped the eggplant. I shall have to throw it away." I would even venture to say it is a satisfactory sound, a satisfactory squishthwack.

This is the sound made when my fist makes contact with Josh's slightly, although not entirely, aroused parts.

Squishthwack.

Josh's arc over my body is interrupted momentarily, and he hangs there in the air, his naked body suspended over mine for the briefest period of time, before he completes his trajectory, now without any sense of direction, intention, or, indeed, consciousness.

Everything happens in slow motion, like they say people experience car accidents, except I'm neither driver nor passenger, I'm just trying to answer the phone, and I watch Josh's head suddenly take on weight and perform like an anchor, diving off the bed and into the floorboards, which actually aren't floorboards since I live in a sound-proof building, so the floor is concrete.

First his head disappears, then his torso, then there's a jarring thud and his body is still for a fraction of a second, his legs straight up and down before the knees buckle and his entire body seems to disappear below the rim of the bed, like sand in an hourglass. I actually think this, "like sand in an hourglass," before I answer the phone.

"Hello," I say.

"Hello," says Simpson.

"Mah jaa!" says Josh.

"What was that?" asks Simpson.

"Josh," I say. "He fell out of bed."

"I see," says Simpson."

"Mah gaw!" says Josh.

"I think he broke his jaw," I say.

"Oh," says Simpson. "Listen, I know this sounds crazy. But I think it's sex."

"Not really," I say. "Sound-proof apartment, concerete floors," I explain.

"Ungh," Josh says.

"Sex," Simpson says. "You, me, Mr. S, we were all having sex, with different people I mean, when the Ganesh came to life."

"Oh," I say.

"Ohhhh," says Josh.

"The Ganesh on TV," Simpson says.

"Right," I say.

ACTION NEWS . . . IN THE RIVER VALLEY

What began as a mystery murder in this quiet riverside valley has turned into a **nasty** story of **eth**nic violence where **no**body—not **even** the media—is safe.

A little over a week ago, **Ac**tion News reporter Josh Conrad broadcast his account of the **In**dian Godfather case. He stayed on to dig deeper into this sinister story.

Well, **this** was Josh Conrad a week ago—and **this** is him today, a **beaten, brutalized** man, his face a **bloody** pulp and covered in medical gauze, his body, **battered** and **broken.**

As investigative journalists, we are prepared to take risks. But **nothing** could have prepared this reporter for meeting Josh Conrad just this morning at Mercy General. He cannot **speak** or **feed** himself because of a broken jaw received during a gang beating he received when following up his story. But even once in hospital, this brave reporter had not seen the end. According to sources, an Indian Godfather henchman came to his private room to deliver a **violent** message. This sadistic gangster dislocated Josh's toe with his bare hand, a torture-procedure called toe-jamming popular with Indian gangs, then proceeded to headbutt him into unconsciousness. If not for the arrival of a nurse on her regular rounds, there is no telling what might have happened to Josh Conrad.

And yet still, police in this community continue to turn a blind eye to the rising ethnic violence that has imposed an un**spo**ken curfew here. Not only do they **refuse** to offer media protection, but they **continue** to insist that Josh Conrad's injuries are a result of a series of unfortunate **"accidents."** Well, I look at Josh Conrad and, while I'm no medical expert, they don't look like the result of any **"accident"** to me. For now, I remain, by Josh's side, on the scene of this brutal landscape. **I'm** Priscilla Lane, **Ac**tion News.

GANESH

We are in a dark place. Sometime during the night, someone, or someones, picked us up from different places. And now we are in a dark place. There are voices, muffled by the sky. A dark sky. We wait.

"What's in the bag, Simpson?" asks a muffled voice.

"You'll see. In a minute, you'll see," says another muffled voice.

There are sounds of fumbling and clicking. Voices emerge, incomplete voices, as if they are far away and all the nuances of pitch are truncated. They are recorded voices, electronic voices. There is light at the top. We can see. We are three.

I look about. I am loose at the bottom of a large shopping bag, lying on my back, face up. I see Ganesh carved in wood, rosewood, I think, nice ornamentation, a part-smile on his face. I see Ganesh of cloth, overstuffed, eyes of sewed-on fabric, pudgier than usual, a single tusk of bulky canvas protruding and bent back by the side of the bag.

I look about. I am standing straight up, facing the other two. Ganesh is lying on the side of his face, looking uncomfortable. He is decorated in blue and green, his vest of red satin adorned with tiny mirrors. Very Indian. Ganesh, I do not know he is Ganesh at first, is curled up in the bottom of the bag. He is barely evident in the third dimension, pressed almost flat on the medallion, silver. His features are not entirely recognizable, but this is Ganesh, and for a moment I think our beltline serpent is with us, come unhinged from one of us, I think, but then I see it's Medallion-Ganesh's chain, fine-linked, nestling in the bag.

I look about. I can see out of one eye only, the other smushed into the side of this paper bag. But right in my face, my one good eye, is Ganesh, smirking ridiculously. He is silver on silver, squatting like me. Pretty guy, I think. Beyond him I can see Ganesh, cherrywood. He's dancing. I like a dancing Ganesh. He's standing straight up and dancing, making me feel all the more undignified. A hand reaches into the bag and removes us, one by one.

I am straightened out, fluffed up, placed on the couch.

I am lifted out carefully, stood near the edge, but not too close to the edge, of an oak coffee table.

I am pulled by my chain, I swing freely, the room whirls, the bag lets go. I come to rest in a palm, a white palm, gentle but strong, I know these things. I am used to leaning on a brown chest, a few sprouts of hair my bed, not too many like I've seen on others, a real jungle, would hate to live in such a mat. The hand is warm, too. My chain dangles between fingers, dripping toward the floor.

"So what's up, Simpson? What is all this?"

"Ganesh. Ganeshes. The wooden one is applewood, I think, made in California. He was in this store down on Centre Street. Picked him up yesterday. The stuffed one was in a box of kids' stuff. Got it at a basement sale just around the corner, saw the sign on the way back from the Oriental Boutique. And the chain in your hand, that's Sandip's. He wears it a lot, sometimes overnight. I'd never really looked at it before. When I told him about my idea, he just took it off and showed it to me."

"What idea? And what's with the videotape?"

"I been thinking, D. It's like you said with Mr. S. He's not acting like a caught felon, trying to wriggle outta the charge. But he's also not acting —"

"Not acting like he's a pyscho, yeah. It's like there's something else, something very weird, going on."

"Uh-huh. So I'm telling 'Dip more about this case, and we start talking about watching TV that night and seeing Ganesh come to life, even though everyone said it was a hoax and all."

"What're you getting at, Simpson? This sounds really far-fetched."

"I know, but listen. 'Dip goes into work the next day, that was two days ago, and he does a web search for Ganesh, just out of interest. He comes across all these sites that are all excited about this milk-drinking thing that came up on TV."

I look over at wood-Ganesh and see that he's just as enthralled as me. Medallion-Ganesh is being rubbed by the thumb of the woman, which he seems to enjoy, but he is also quite excited about all this news about us.

"So there're Hindu idols drinking milk. I still don't get it. What about our case?"

"I'm getting to that. On a couple of sites, 'Dip finds people talking about Ganeshes moving their trunks, actually reaching out for the milk. Yeah, he figures like I do, they're off their rockers, seeing what they wanna see. Anyway, so he's telling me all this at breakfast yesterday . . ."

I remember that. Her thumb is a bit calloused but still quite smooth underneath. Funny, that. I remember Sandip putting me on in the morning, not too carefully I might add, the clasp didn't quite hold.

". . . and we're starting to laugh at all this, people really make a thing outta this. . . ."

Sandip was sitting down in the kitchen. I had to struggle to turn around, which happens a lot, and I like Sandip and his warm chest, it's comforting listening to his breathing, but I wanted to face out, see the morning. I managed to twist around just in time to see that enormous spoon coming up, past me on his chest, overhead to his lips. That spoon. A bunch of circular wheaty looking things floating around in what I thought was the most delicious sea of milk I had ever seen. Well, the spoon went down again, and I followed it, first with my eyes, and then, with a fairly monumental effort of telekinesis, all that work to unhook a loosely fastened clasp, and down I went. Plop. Right into the bowl. Oh, what a glorious swim and drink that was.

". . . and that," he's pointing at me in her hand, "that Ganesh tore itself off 'Dip's neck and went straight for his bowl of cereal, right into it."

"Simpson, let me be the first to tell you, you've gone round the bend. Goodbye." She stands and starts to walk toward the door, me still in her hand.

"No, wait, D. That's just the start. Sandip also read me a post from a woman who had worked on the *Mahabharata*, the film that Peter Brooks made. Look, it's on right now. See this part here?"

Simpson is pointing to the television with the excitement of a two-year-old.

"I see a guy with a very badly-designed elephant head."

"Yeah, but this woman said they had to stop in the middle of filming one day, cuz this guy, the guy with the elephant head, got it stuck. This part here, I've watched it over and over."

"Who's the old guy?"

"Vyasa, the sage whose story Ganesh writes down. Look there, did ya see that?"

Simpson grabs the remote control and backs up the tape. He hits play and then pause. The image is frozen. We look at each other and at Ganesh on the screen. In between the woman's fingers, Ganesh struggles to get a look at the screen.

For this frame, and only this frame, the ragtag and very fake-looking elephant head has been transformed. He is us. We are him. And from underneath his shifting, breathing trunk, in the corner of his lip, is a tiny drool of milk.

DELILAH

Hi, Josh. How ya doin'? Hurts, huh. Don't try to speak.
Doctor says you're mouth'll be wired shut for four weeks.
Did they already tell you that? Don't try to speak. Just nod
or shake your head. Oh, it hurts to shake your head? Oh.
Listen, I'm sorry about your jaw. Comedy of errors, I guess.
Well, not a very funny comedy for you, huh? Guess this pretty
much puts you outta commission for the rest of this story,
huh? I mean, you can edit and fake all the standups you want,
but unless you get some sound techie to scramble old audio
tape and make it sound like you're talking, looks like that's
it. I am sorry. I didn't mean to poke you like that. It was just
that the phone was ringing. Instinctual reaction. Like that.
Too bad, though, looks like we've got this major break on the
case. Really weird, but I'm starting to buy into it. I tell ya,
this is one story that would make the networks fall over
themselves outbidding each other for you. If only you could
report it, eh? Them's the breaks. Sorry, bad choice of words.

Oh, Josh, speaking of bad choices, I gotta tell ya something. Whatever we had, Josh, and I know and you know it
wasn't much, but still, whatever we had is over. 'Fraid so.
Like I told you once, I don't really like you, so I can't tell you
this shit about you being a good person and how you deserve
someone special or nothing. As a matter of fact, not to
offend or nothing, but I think you're a class-A jerk and I pity
anyone who gets involved with you. Thing is, I don't think
you'll change, not that I ever did, but still, I thought I should
tell you this face to face. Oh, and the sex. The first three
times, maybe four, it wasn't bad, really. But I think that may

have been cuz of the newness of it all. After that, serious downhill.

So, ciao, Josh. Stay outta trouble. Oh, one more thing, I brought you a goodbye present. It's a Ganesh, just a little sandalwood one. He's supposed to remove obstacles out of people's way, or sometimes put them there, I dunno how that works. Anyway, I'll just set him down here, okay?

Bye, Josh.

GANESH

I am sitting on top of a television monitor that is suspended by two large cables from the ceiling. The monitor, and me, face a hospital bed in which a very injured-looking young man lies. His eyes are all puffy and discoloured; his nose is hidden beneath a mound of bandages and plastic things; his mouth is wired firmly shut so he looks a little like a robot on one of those 1950s television shows. I regret that I am sitting on top of the television here because from this position I can hear, but not see what's on TV.

The patient looks miserable. He uses the remote control to change the channel.

Someone comes into the room. A nice, if a bit scruffy-looking, Indian boy. He is wearing a black leather jacket. He looks a bit upset.

"You, Mr. Josh Conrad. They told me you were in here. I came looking for you. You told me I would be on TV, that people would see me on TV and would think, 'Oh, look, Amrit is on TV, he must be very important person.' Mr. Conrad, you told me this, isn't it? Mr. Conrad, where is my face on TV? Do you see my face on TV? I am very angry with you, Mr. Conrad. You do not treat people this way, telling them one thing and then doing entirely another thing. This is not good."

The young man pauses. The patient, this Josh Conrad, looks at him helplessly. The young man comes closer to the bed so that he is almost touching it. He looks very stern, but I can tell he won't hurt Josh Conrad.

"I came to really give you a piece of my mind, Mr. Conrad, and I hope you have learned your lesson. You make it so that I get my hopes all high and think if I am a gang member people will address me with respect. You are a bad man, Mr. Conrad. I do not like you."

"Medicine time," a chimey voice says, startling all three of us considerably.

I almost slip off the television.

Josh Conrad's eyes grow wide.

The young Indian boy, whose back is to the door when the nurse comes in, gets the worst of it. He pivots around in fear. He is not good at pivoting and he begins to lose his balance. His feet come out from under him. His legs splay. He reaches out with his left hand and grabs only empty air. He reaches out with his right hand.

Josh Conrad has been lying close to the edge of the bed. He doesn't find hospital beds particularly comfortable, so he has moved around until he has found the least uncomfortable position, in which one foot, his left one, sticks ever so slightly off the side of the bed. It rests there, his foot, a protrusion and an ever-so-handy handle.

The young Indian boy has completely lost his footing. As a matter of fact, I can see the soles of both his shoes as his rump hurtles floorward. A moment before he hits the floor, his right hand finds a handle. His right hand grips, in what some would call a death grip, and his full weight is transferred to his right hand and, by extension, to the handle.

The most protrusive part of this handle is Josh Conrad's big toe. It is this toe that the young Indian boy grabs to break his fall. This does not succeed in breaking his fall, however. He still lands, very hard, on his rump and bruises his tailbone. As he lands, he feels a very elastic-sounding snap come from his right hand, a sound that is quickly followed by the arrival of four toes and a foot onto the floor where he now sits, all being led by a big toe, quite flappy now, which is tightly gripped in his fingers. This is followed by the rest of Josh Conrad's body, twisted off the bed and turned to land, face-first, on the crown of the young Indian boy's head.

Hospitals can provide such obstacles to recovery.

GANESH

"It's bells and whistles, Simpson. Strange footage, a flicker of light, and you're making it sound like this film – from what year – is our case."

"There's more."

"Of course there's more. There's always more. This is too much more."

Simpson leaves the room.

Delilah sits there, her warm fingers still pressing into my belly, and I can tell she thinks she should leave but will not. "I'm going to give Josh the heave," she yells into the other room, hoping to change the subject. "Just thought you might like to know."

There is no verbal response but I know Simpson is still there, in the kitchen, because I hear the fridge open and close. We three are suddenly more attentive.

"I took him to the hospital before coming here, y'know," she yells. "I'm pretty sure he broke his jaw. Did a –"

Simpson comes back into the room carrying a large bowl. It's the cat's bowl. I recognize it from the times Sandip has bent down to fill it up with catfood and I've dangled over the meaty smell for precarious seconds. Delilah lowers her voice as Simpson re-enters.

"– header right off the bed. I'm afraid it's my fault. I accidentally hit him and – what are you doing?"

Simpson has laid the bowl down right in front of the TV. I can see now, we can all see, it's full of milk, still frothing from the pour.

"We're going to wait," says Simpson, sitting on the couch beside her.

"For how long?"

"Until it happens," Simpson says. He picks up the remote control, flicks the VCR off and turns to a news channel.

JUDGE McECHERN

Judge McEchern wants this to be over.

His courtroom has turned into a zoo and nobody seems to care. It's business as usual for everyone except him.

Today the accused will take the stand in his own defence. Judge McEchern has already decided to find him guilty so he doesn't see what good this will do, but then the rest of the court doesn't know that Judge McEchern has made up his mind and is not taking copious notes anymore but is actually occupying himself by trying to finish the crossword puzzle from last weekend's *New York Times*. He has never finished a *Times* crossword puzzle and he is determined to do so this time. However, to keep up appearances, Judge McEchern listens carefully to the tone of people's voices as they testify, although he largely ignores the content. If they change their tone markedly, Judge McEchern looks up in apparent interest in what they're saying and sometimes looks over to the person in the witness stand and either nods or frowns, depending on what he thinks is called for. Sometimes, Judge McEchern, without actually looking up, will utter courtly commands, like "Please get on with it, Mr. Khosla," or "Let's get back to the pertinent evidence, *Miz* Block," without ever really listening to what either of them, or anyone else, is saying. Judge McEchern is actually quite proud of himself that he can discern wasted breath without listening to exactly what words or cogent ideas those wasted breaths are formulating.

"The court calls Sam Sribhaiman to the stand."

Judge McEchern watches the foreign accused, looking relaxed but confused, approach the bench. He begins to turn the wrong way, toward the empty jury box, before the court clerk signals that he should actually climb onto the witness stand.

Sheesh, thinks Judge McEchern, and, he momentarily practices, silently of course, the remonstrative tone he will use when finding the accused guilty of such a heinous crime. Thirty-six down is a five-letter word for Macintosh ending with "e".

The accused is sworn in and the legal aid lawyer rises to begin his questioning. Judge McEchern will pay more attention as soon as he finishes this block and he has only three more words to get. Computer is too long and besides it's spelled differently. Apple, he writes in.

"Will you tell the court, Dr. Sribhaiman, your place of residence and your occupation?"

Judge McEchern always hates the initial part of questioning anyway, always trying to prove beyond a reasonable doubt such facile details as how someone spells his name and whether he lives in the upstairs apartment or basement suite of whatever address. Eighty-eight across, five letter word ending in "a", destructive deity. God is too short, Judge McEchern thinks, remembering all his Sunday school teachings about floods and locusts and stuff.

"And can you tell me, Dr. Sribhaiman, if you recognize this particular item that I hold in my hand right now?"

"Yes," says the witness. "It belongs to me."

"Let the record show the accused has identified Crown exhibit 'A'," says the legal aid lawyer.

Zeus fits, almost, and he has those thunderbolts, but the word's supposed to end in "a", maybe the word down is wrong, what's the number, thirty-two.

"And can you tell the court if this item, this sword, was in your possession on the evening of Tuesday, October the 29th?"

"No. I mean, I don't know. I mean, I didn't know it was missing until after, until later."

Judge McEchern, in a careless moment of inattention to his crossword puzzle, hears this comment. Ignorance is no excuse, he hums to himself, guilty guilty guilty and stupid too for taking the stand if you can't lie your way out of a paper bag. Thirty-two down is Rocker, Frank, five letters, gotta be Zappa, for sure, and that goes with eighty-four across, five letters, Marx bro', has to be Zeppo. So the a, the second a in Zappa, last letter in destructive deity, stands.

"Dr. Sribhaiman, could you please tell the court where you acquired this sword?"

"I got it in India. Well, actually, it was given to me. Near Mysore in the south of India, there was this guy by the roadside, I thought he was a cobra-charmer, but he just wanted to give me this thing, this shiv."

That still leaves this destructive deity, five letters, ending in "a". What are all those names for the devil?

"And when this person gave you this item, this sword, Dr. Sribhaiman, did he tell you why he gave it to you?"

"Well, like, he said he was getting sick, needed somebody else to take care of it."

"Someone like you?"

"That's what he said."

Maybe it's someone else in that Greek pantheon. Thor, he broke things up with that hammer of his. Athena, now there's one that ends with an "a", but no, too long, and wasn't she the goddess of wisdom or hunting or something?

"And did he say where he acquired the sword?"

"Well, not exactly."

"Not exactly?"

Maybe it's the word for God in another language, maybe it's one of those Mediterranean things, like Goda or whatever.

"Well, he told me it belonged to – to Lord Shiva."

"Shiva!" Judge McEchern fairly jumps out of his judge chair as he shouts out the name.

"Your Honour?" says the legal aid lawyer.

"Your Worship?" says the Crown prosecutor.

"Uh, yes, Shiva," says Judge McEchern, writing it down as if he were taking detailed notes but putting each letter in its own box. "S-h-i-v-a."

"One last question," says the legal aid lawyer. "Is it not true, Dr. Sribhaiman, that you were unaccounted for for three entire days during which time the 'elephant and head' incident took place, and further to that, is it not true that this very same Lord Shiva for whom you were safekeeping his sword, incarnated himself in your body to re-enact a sacred and important mission duly recorded in the Mahabharata?"

"Um. I guess so," says Dr. Sribhaiman.

Judge McEchern, having finished pencilling in Shiva's name, is now staring at the legal aid lawyer as if he were naked or on fire or slowly beginning to melt before everyone's eyes.

Judge McEchern is rather concerned with the leaps of assumption made by that last question and is wondering if he is the only one.

"Objection," says the Crown.

"Mr. Khosla," begins Judge McEchern.

"I have no further questions," says the legal aid lawyer, heading back to his desk purposefully and proceeding to pull the top off a shoe box sitting there. "Just one request. Dr. Sribhaiman, would you please catch these balls as I throw them to you?"

He does not wait for a response. He picks up a blue and white beanbag ball, the kind jugglers use when they're practicing. He throws it at Mr. S. Mr. S. catches it in one hand.

"What is the meaning of this?" Judge McEchern explodes.

The legal aid lawyer takes another blue and white beanbag ball and throws it at Mr. S. Mr. S. catches it with his other hand.

Judge McEchern is excited. He will be able to lay another contempt charge, one that will stick for sure, and the best part is he gets to nail this foreign-looking legal aid lawyer who has that ridiculous looking ponytail that's bobbing up and down even now as he tosses ball after ball after ball at the accused, his own client for god's sake. Judge McEchern was wrong about his courtroom turning into a zoo – it's turning into a circus, juggling acts and all.

"Mr. Khosla!" yells Judge McEchern. The legal aid lawyer fires balls three, four, five at the man in the witness stand.

"Mr. Khosla, it is with extreme pleasure that I find you in contempt of this court!" The legal aid lawyer is apparently running out of juggling balls, because he turns fully toward the witness stand now, the last three balls clutched to his chest. He throws them with precision. Six.

"Mr. Khosla. I have found you in contempt."

Seven.

"Mr. Khosla, I am left with no option but to have you removed!"

Eight.

"Bailiff, remove this man. Take him from this courtroom and put him behind bars."

The bailiff doesn't move. The legal aid lawyer, puffing mildly from his eight overhand throws, doesn't move. The Crown prosecutor, her hand caught up by her collar, doesn't move. Nobody in the entire gallery moves. Everyone is staring at the witness stand.

Judge McEchern does not like the look of this. Judge McEchern turns his body to face the witness stand. The accused is sitting there passively, his face in a wide smile. In each hand he holds one of the blue and white beanbag juggling balls thrown to him by the legal aid lawyer.

In each hand.

One, two, three, four, five, six, seven, eight.

SIDDHI

"Wanna go out for dinner?"

"Tonight? Sure."

"'Kay, let's get ready."

"What, now? It's only two o'clock."

"It's a long drive up north."

"North where?"

"To my parents'."

"Oh."

"Well? Let's get ready."

"Greg? Um. Maybe we should wait."

"Nah. Let's get ready."

VIGHNESVARA

I am in the forest, having followed the river down from the mountain town. I am idling my time away, trying to think of ways to convince the court that there has been no murder, there has been no crime, and all is right with the world. Coyote has told me to testify, which is a good idea and I shall do that, but there has to be something more.

I sit down in the forest by the river and scratch the top of my head with my trunk.

I am interrupted by a snort. I look up. Water still dripping down his chin, having raised his hairy head from a pool of water eddying in from the river, a large ungulate glares at me.

"You're not an elk," says the ungulate.

"No," I say to the ungulate. "I'm an elephant." I think about my conversation with Coyote and decide to be clearer. "I am part person and part elephant, Mr. Ungulate," I say.

"What did you call me?" asks Ungulate.

"Ungulate," I say. "An ungulate is a hoofed animal. You have hoofs. Therefore, you are an ungulate, Ungulate."

"I'm not an ungulate," says Not-Ungulate. "I'm an elk."

"You can be an ungulate and an elk," I offer.

"No, I'm an elk," says Elk. His tongue slides out to slurp some water drops hanging on to his hairy chin. "I'm an elk. And you're not an elk."

"That's right, I'm an eleph — " I decide not to continue and nod instead.

Elk nods back and lowers his head to resume drinking.

There is something intriguing about this Elk character. He reminds me of someone, but I can't quite place him. I think he might be able to help me.

"Elk?"

He ignores me.

"Yoohoo. Elk?"

He still ignores me.

"Hey, Elk. ELKELKELK."

He looks up, dripping little rivulets from his chin. "You," says Elk. "You are not an elk." He goes back to his drinking so that all I can see of him is his huge rack, bobbing up and down, all twelve points of it.

"No, I'm not an elk, I admitted that," I say. "Can we talk anyway?"

"Nope," says Elk, not lifting his head from the water. "Can't talk. You're no elk. Can only talk to elk."

"Why, that's ridiculous," I think to myself.

"Why, that's ridiculous," I say to Elk. "You're being ridiculous."

"You're being ridiculous," says Elk. "I'm being Elk."

For some reason, I really want to engage this Elk in conversation.

Maybe if I say, "Ahem, Elk? I, too, am being Elk."

Elk looks up. He glares at me. He snorts. If elk can grin, and I'm not entirely sure they can, Elk grins. "No, you're not."

"Yes I am. I am Elk," I say.

"Prove it," says Elk.

Now, apart from a few grumpy words, I'm not exactly sure what elk sound like, although on my way out to the mountain centre, before I made my way downriver to the forest, I passed through rolling prairies inhabited by great herds of what appeared to be elk-like creatures, and I *did* hear them calling to one another in various degrees of earnestness and urgency. I think I'll try this out on Elk.

"Moooo."

Elk glares at me.

"Moooooooo."

"You're not elk," sneers Elk, that is, if elk can sneer. "You are cow." Elk does not hide his derision when he says "cow."

"How can you tell?" I ask.

Elk shakes his head slowly. "Elk do not go 'mooo.' Elk go 'ooooo.'"

"Oh," I say.

"No, no, not 'oh,' 'oooo.'"

"Ooooo?"

"Yeah," says Elk. "Now, piss off, cow."

"I'm not cow. I'm Vighnesvara, remover of obstacles."

"You are cow, giver of milk, eater of grasslands, and, worst of all, willing self-sacrificer to the slaughterhouses. Wimps."

"Well then, Elk, how can I be more like Elk?"

Elk glares at me again, obviously not excited about entertaining a cow in conversation. He sighs. "Okay," he says. "But I'll only say this once. First, twitch your nose like this. Smell danger. Run from it. Second, open your ears like this. Listen for the hunters. All they want is your rack to hang on their walls. Hunters. Hmmph. No better than cows, really. Third, keep your eyes alert, especially at night, so when it's your time you can jump out onto their highways and stare into the bright eyes of their stupid caravans hurtling at stupid speeds in the dark so the last thing they see before the big crunch are your elk eyes staring them down. Huh."

"That's what being Elk is all about?"

"That," says Elk, "that and rutting."

"Oh," I say. "Thank you Elk. I think you've given me an idea."

"Get lost, cow," says Elk.

"Moo," I say. And I depart.

SIDDHI

"Do they know I'm coming?"

"Yup."

"Do they know who I am?"

"Nope."

"Do they think I'm white?"

"Nope."

"Did you come out to them and not tell me?"

"Nope."

"Aren't you scared?"

"Yup."

"Why now?"

"Why not?"

"Greg, is there anything I should *not* talk to your parents about?"

"How long have we been driving?"

"About fifteen minutes."

"Shit, that only gives me a little more than three hours to tell you what you probably shouldn't say."

"Bad as all that, huh?"

"Do not talk to my parents about abortion. Do not talk to my parents about free trade. Do not talk to my parents about First Nations rights or law. Do not talk to my parents about who they voted for in the last election – municipal, provincial, or federal – you won't like their answers. Do not talk to my parents about welfare. Do not talk to my parents about any social cause you have ever or are ever likely to be involved in. Do not talk to my parents about environmental issues, legal or otherwise. Do not talk to my parents about immigration policy. Do not talk to my parents about the

Third World. Do not talk to my father about gun control.
Do not talk to my mother about feminism."

"Greg?"

"Yeah."

"I guess Queer theory is right out, then, eh?"

GANESH

I have been sitting in Greg's and Sandip's kitchen for four days. It was Greg who found me, a bit dust-covered, but quite happy really, sitting in the back of Mr. Singh's restaurant. Greg fell in love with me right away. Couldn't take his eyes off me, dragged his friend Delilah over to look at me, my finely chiselled face and body. My soapstone body has weathered a few storms in its two hundred years, that's true, but I still got the look. It was Mrs. Singh's brother-in-law who brought me back, lugged me over in that steamer trunk, must be ten years ago now. But Greg was looking at me with such wonder that when he asked Mr. Singh where one could find such a beautiful Ganesh and that he wanted one, needed one, just like this for a very special person, it was Mrs. Singh who intervened and said, "Lalji, let him take it, we have had it long enough, and look at his face, bucha, he wants it for love only."

And so Greg brought me back home and I was sitting in their kitchen for four days and now I'm laying down in the backseat of Greg's car, watching the sky go by as I have for the past three-and-a-half hours. The car makes several turns and stops and finally Greg turns off the engine. He and Sandip talked about Greg's parents for the first hour and haven't said much of anything for the rest of the ride.

Greg gets out. Sandip gets out.

"Well, hello there, ol' man," shouts Greg.

"Ha-hah, howya doin', boy!" I can hear Greg and his father hugging and slapping each other on the back.

"Dad, this is Sandip."

"Sandip, good ta meet ya."

"Nice to meet you, too, Mr. Simpson."

"Ha-hah. Mr. Simpson. Call me Dave. Dave it is. Dave."

"Okay. Dave."

Greg opens up the back door and begins to heft me out. I am heavy, even for him, and Sandip grabs my bottom half. Carried like that to the house, I can see only their faces and they are glancing nervously over at each other.

"So far so good," says Greg.

"So far," echoes Sandip.

"Whoo-ee, that's some doorstop there, Gregor," says Dave.

"Well, actually, it's a present for you and Mom. It's a statue of —"

"Of Ganesh," says Dave, nodding as Greg and Sandip set me down, as luck would have it, by the edge of the door. "I'm not dense, Gregor. It's a wonderful present. Beautiful."

Sandip adjusts my position so I can see clear into the kitchen down one hall and into the living room past the foyer. This is a good place to be.

"Hello, hello, hello," says a voice coming closer down the hall. Greg's mother, I assume.

"Hi, Ma."

"Hi, Gregor. It was such a wonderful surprise to hear you'd be coming up to see us this evening. Wonderful. This must be Sandip."

"Sandip, this is my mom, Gillian."

"Hi, Gillian."

"Hi, Sandip. Well, come in, come in, let's eat."

I can see them all at the kitchen table. Gillian's back is to me and so is Greg's, but I can see both Sandip's and Dave's faces quite clearly. I sit back and relax. Dinner is some type of partly-cooked meat. And big fluffy mashed potatoes. And something green, beans probably. They spend the dinner-time talking about work, Greg's, Sandip's, Dave's, Gillian's. Greg talks about cop things but doesn't mention the big Ganesh case that he's always talking about at home. Sandip talks about what it's like to be a legal aid lawyer in a busy court of Queen's Bench. Dave talks about farming and how difficult it was and that's why he got out of it and started managing the co-op instead. Gillian talks about the three days a week she works at the accountant's office which doubles as a notary public and she wonders how different it must be to be doing what Sandip does. This is what they talk about. After dinner Gillian brings out a large cheesecake she has made from a neighbour's strawberries, frozen for a couple of months now so they're not as fresh as when they were picked but oh they were good when they were fresh. They all have a piece of cheesecake and Dave helps himself to another piece allowing that this is a special occasion because his son has come for dinner and has brought his friend.

"So, Sandip," Dave says, "you Gregor's partner?"

Sandip has a piece of cheesecake about a quarter of an inch from his mouth. He holds it there. "Sorry?"

Dave looks embarrassed. "I mean, do you work together at all. I mean, like cops and lawyers and stuff?"

"Oh," says Sandip, letting the fork enter his mouth now.

"Oh," echoes Greg, although he is not involved in this conversation and his father duly ignores him.

"Uh-huh. Some. Not all the time, but we have the occasional common case."

"I see," says Dave. "Do you smoke, Sandip?"

Sandip looks at Dave. Sandip looks at Greg. He has the occasional cigarette, but he is not sure what to say. This was not one of the items on the "do not talk about" list. He sees Greg nod surreptitiously.

"Uh, yeah, sometimes."

"Ha-hah," says Dave. "Had ta get permission from my boy, eh? C'mon, let's you and me go have a smoke on the front porch, let these two non-smokers keep each other company."

"Okay," says Sandip. He looks at Greg on the way out and smiles slightly. Then, as he passes me, he smiles again. Dave and Sandip go past me and out the front door. They close the storm door behind them, but leave the main door slightly ajar so I can hear them.

"Nice night," says Sandip, and I can tell he's taking one of the cigarettes Dave has offered to him.

"Yup. Nice night for November." I hear a lighter flick. "Gonna get colder though, soon."

"Yeah. Yeah, I guess."

"Say, Sandip?"

"Yeah, Dave?"

"My son happy?"

"Um. Yes. Yes, I think so."

"Yeah. Me too. Know what I think?"

"Um, no?"

"Think it's you that makes him so happy."

"Oh."

"Been together for a while, then?"

"Sorry? I mean – I mean, yeah. Yes. Two years. We've been together for two years."

"Ha-hah. Thought so. Told Gill somethin' musta happened about two years back, cuz all of a sudden Gregor was all lightened up and stuff. Gill said she thought maybe it was cuz he got along with his new partner and I said it probably did have somethin' ta do with partners, but not at work. Ha-hah. That's what I said."

"I see."

"He's a good boy, that Gregor."

"Yes, he is."

"You take care of him, okay?"

"Okay."

"And, hey, Sandip? That sure is a fine-looking Ganesh you and Gregor brought for us. Fine-looking."

SIDDHI

"It's about vestiges," says Sandip.

"Vestiges," says Delilah.

"Vestiges," says Simpson.

"Vestiges," says Mr. S.

"Tell 'em, Sam," says Sandip.

Sandip and his client, Mr. S, are sitting across from Delilah and her partner, Simpson. Sandip has called this meeting. He thinks the investigating officers should hear what his client has to say.

"Um, it's hard to describe. Vestiges, I'm usin' that term ta describe a sorta residual cosmic energy, so ta speak."

"Cosmic energy," says Delilah

"Cosmic energy," says Simpson.

"Yeah, cosmic energy," says Mr. S. "Call it supernatural or transcendent or spiritual energy, if ya will. It's, well, it's, like, cosmic."

"I got this idea," Sandip breaks in, "when you, Greg, started talking about sex. You told me that all of us had been engaged in sex directly prior to the elephant-event on late night television. Like there was some sort of connection."

"Wait a second," interrupts Delilah. "First off, what makes us so important, and second off, that late-night show is pre-recorded at, like, seven o'clock in the evening. How could we be 'responsible,' if that's what yer getting at, for something that's already happened?"

Mr. S is getting excited. "No, no, that's exactly it," he says. Everyone stares at him. "Y'see, it's about slippages of time, a falling apart of cause and effect. Sure, the show's recorded like six hours before we see it, but it's like observin' the cat in the box, like is it live or dead, I mean, ya can't know unless ya look and yer act of looking makes it happen, y'know?"

Delilah and Simpson look at Mr. S and then at each other. They both suddenly realize, not understanding a word Mr. S has just said, why he's a professor.

"What Mr. S is trying to say," says Sandip patiently, "is that certain things are simply not bound by rules of physics. Ganesh comes to life on *Late Night* because of residual, vestigial cosmic energy. It doesn't matter which happens first: one causes the other, so to speak. Our sexual activity, brought on by the cosmic play of Shiva and Parvati, reflect and produce the 'coming to life' of Ganesh on TV."

"Jeez, I think I get this," says Simpson.

"Um," says Delilah, "but – are you trying to tell me, Sandip, I mean honestly, that this is Shiva?" She is staring at Mr. S, who just shrugs.

"No, no," says Sandip. "It's more of a temporary incarnating of Shiva in Mr. S." He says this with a finality as if this explains everything.

"It's sorta like a temporary armed occupation," says Mr. S, shifting from metaphysical to military metaphors. "Shiva inhabits my body to cavort with his, my, consort, Parvati, to re-create their son Ganesh. Oh, did I mention that Shiva is also known as Kalasamhara, the destroyer of Time?

"With this creation," continues Sandip, "goes the vestigial leftovers, kinda peppered through different periods in time: a film actor in the Mahabharata becomes the real Ganesh for a moment, in body if not in spirit; the sexual activity of Shiva and Parvati are reflected in our own, particularly those who are somehow most closely connected to the 'vestiges,' like elephant bodies and boy-god's heads; Ganeshes 'round the world first start sipping milk, then, if the timing's right and enough vestigial energy is floating about, they become Ganesh in elephant body and spirit. It's really very simple."

"Simple," says Delilah.

"Simple," says Simpson.

"Simple," says Mr. S.

"So I asked you here," says Sandip, "for a couple of reasons. One's a simple confirmation: Greg, remember that night, before the sex I mean, and you said you'd had a lousy day and just wanted to sleep?"

"Uh, yeah."

"Yeah. And remember I said that was cool, I had a ton of briefs to get through by the next morning?"

"Yeah."

"Yet we had sex. Not great sex, mind you, but sex. For no reason, just a thing about, well, sex. Desire."

"So?" says Simpson, a bit uncomfortable that his private life is being discussed openly with his partner, his lover, and his lover's client.

"So, Delilah, you too?"

"Hmm?"

"You too, right, you had sex right before the television thing."

"Well, yeah, sorta."

"And, like ya told Greg, it wasn't that you really wanted to, and, if my guess is right, this Josh Conrad wasn't particularly into it either."

Delilah looks cross. "Whaddya mean 'wasn't into it'?"

"No insult, Delilah, but that's the truth, right?"

"Well, yeah, I guess. Yeah. Josh wanted to do an exclusive interview with me, something about the 'Woman Who Is Working Day and Night to Break the Indian Godfather Case.' I don't know what happened then. We just kinda looked at each other, and that was it, we were off. But what does this prove?"

"Maybe nothing. Maybe nothing at all," says Sandip. "But just maybe."

Sandip leans down and pulls out a thick file folder from his briefcase, tosses it on the table. Delilah opens it up and begins to peruse the many pieces of paper, all of them downloaded from the Internet and printed on legal size sheets, many of them not even in English.

"And you," says Sandip to his client. "D'you remember yet how your sex life was on the night in question?"

Mr. S clasps his hands in front of him tightly. He is trying to remember, to be helpful, it's just that everything gets so blurry. Parvati, that kid.

"Sorry," he says, running his fingers through his hair in frustration, "it's just that everything's so vague."

But no one is listening to him anymore.

Sandip stares at Mr. S.

Simpson stares at Mr. S.

Simpson prods Delilah with his elbow, causing her to look up from her reading and she, too, stares at Mr. S.

"What?" says Mr. S, still running his fingers through his hair. He looks down and sees that both his hands are still firmly clasped on the table.

VIGHNESVARA

They're getting closer. Humans are incredibly resourceful beasts. And this court thing wouldn't be half bad if they weren't always so darned concerned about the truth.

Stories are so much more interesting. So much truer than truth, come to think of it, so a truly logical mind would prefer stories to bland, this-is-the-way-it-actually-happened truths.

But people *will* be people, dreadfully tied to chronologies, as if time was its own version of truth.

I've invaded this courtroom fiasco so many times just to straighten things out with my own little story, and everything's going along fine, or would, if it weren't for that pesky, squinty, old judge. I have the feeling he's not always paying attention.

Hey Judge! Your Woooorship. Yo.

See. Never listens.

JUDGE McECHERN

Judge McEchern looks up with a start.

The legal aid lawyer, engrossed in his cross-examination of a university cleaning woman, continues to question her, oblivious to the fact that Judge McEchern, to the rest of the courtroom, looks like an elk caught in the headlights of someone's car.

"And, Mrs. Dhaliwallah, can you be absolutely certain that Dr. Sribhaiman had not been in his office for two days, the 29th and 30th of October?"

"No, not certainly," says the witness quietly.

"What was that?" says Judge McEchern, broken from his reverie.

"I said, no, I could not," repeats Mrs. Dhaliwallah.

Judge McEchern peers down from his bench into the witness stand. "Who are you?" he says, snorting ever so softly.

"I am Mrs. Dhaliwallah," says Durga Dhaliwallah.

"You're not a judge," says Judge McEchern.

"No," says Durga Dhaliwallah. "I am not a judge." She smiles at Judge McEchern and nods wisely.

"You're no judge," says Judge McEchern sharply. He looks up at the courtroom and clears his throat. "Can only talk to judges," says Judge McEchern.

"Excuse me?" says the Crown Prosecutor.

"I'm sorry?" says the legal aid lawyer.

But Judge McEchern is off again, staring into the distance, his pink ears pricking up through his somewhat mussed up straight, grey hair. He looks *exactly* like an elk caught in someone's headlights, think several people in the courtroom including the Crown Prosecutor, a couple of witnesses, some casual observers, and three members of the media, one of whom is a sketch artist who unconsciously begins to add a bit of elk hair to her almost-finished rendition of Judge McEchern. Elk hair and little budding antlers where his ears should be.

"Didn't anyone hear that?" says Judge McEchern, turning his head this way and that, straining to catch the next sound.

Nobody answers. They are all afraid this is one of Judge McEchern's rhetorical question ploys to draw someone into a contempt charge, especially since everyone knows he's only got a bit of time to match and break his own record and everyone also knows how badly he wants to do this. But Judge McEchern does not repeat his question, and still tilts his head this way and that, so much so that the sketch artist begins to re-shape the eyes of Judge McEchern, making them, oh, a bit larger and doe-like.

Finally, the Crown Prosecutor speaks: "Hear what, Your Honour?" she says, quite consciously not pulling on her collar.

"It sounded –" Judge McEchern begins, staring now up at the very top left rear corner of the courtroom where someone has forgotten to clean so there's a noticeable spider's web forming, noticeable even to Judge McEchern's eyes, and he makes a mental note to mention this to his clerk if he ever remembers to write this down, "– it sounded like an elephant trumpeting."

There is silence in the courtroom, one of many over the last few weeks, usually occasioned by Judge McEchern's sighting, hearing, or feeling of an elephant presence.

"Um," says the legal aid lawyer, "if it please the court, the defence requests a brief recess. I could continue my cross later this afternoon," he says, adding quietly, "after an itsy-bitsy judgey nap."

"Hm?" says Judge McEchern. "Oh, very well. If you wish." Then he looks down on the brown woman in the witness stand who stares up at him patiently.

"Who are you," he thinks, "aren't you the one who spent half an hour talking in goojruddy just recently, and, if so, what are you doing back as a Crown witness anyway?"

"Thank you, Mrs. Ummhmm," he says. "You are excused for now."

JUDGE McECHERN

Judge McEchern is discussing identity politics and post-colonial theory. He doesn't know much about identity politics – he is a self-made man, he tells himself and anyone who will listen, and he is an individual, a self-made individual, that's all the identity politics that he cares to discuss – and postcolonial theory, well, postcolonial theory is surely something out in left field, way out in left field, and really the little he has read about colonization has convinced him that, despite all the current debate and argumentation, colonizers did, after all, bring a lot of good things into the lives of those they colonized. Like protecting their women from their men. Like paved roads, he says. And flush toilets.

What concerns Judge McEchern most greatly, however, is that he is discussing identity politics and postcolonial theory with an elephant-headed witness.

"Let's put it this way," says the witness. "If you consider yourself self-defined, Your Honour, and I, sitting before you, am the outer limits upon which your self defines itself, then you are dependent on me, that which you define yourself against negatively, for your existence."

There is a hush in the gallery.

Judge McEchern frowns. He is not sure what the witness is saying, but he is sure he doesn't like it. Judge McEchern has an idea.

"You're telling me that you, by your remarkable difference, define me, who and what I am?" he asks.

"More or less," and the elephant head bobs up and down.

"Ah, but you aren't real," says Judge McEchern confidently. "I have created you, you're a figment of my dementia, ha. So there. Talk your way out of that one!"

"You mean, I don't exist?"

"Precisely."

"Well, then, if I am not, if I have not been produced by your self-definition as your negative other, well then, 'the non-being of the other challenges the very terms of the definition.'"

"Whose definition?"

"Yours," says the elephant-headed witness.

And he vanishes.

Judge McEchern looks around. The courtroom is changing, dissolving. Faces are becoming different, older, stouter. Judge McEchern sees everyone turning into him.

"What's the meaning of this?" shouts Judge McEchern.

"I demand an explanation," shouts the Judge McEchern tugging at his collar.

"What sort of trick is this?" shouts the Judge McEchern typing in the court proceedings.

"This is my courtroom," shouts the Judge McEchern with a tiny two-inch ponytail that begins to turn grey and brittle as he speaks.

"Stop it," shouts the Judge McEchern at his judge table which is starting to dissolve and transmogrify into the same type of plasticky card-table that is beginning to appear in front of all the other Judge McEcherns.

"Stop it," he shouts again.

"Stop it," the Judge McEcherns shout in unison, banging their hands on top of their rattly cardtables because none of them appear to have their gavels within reach.

The elephant-headed one reappears on the witness stand.

Judge McEchern reverts back to a collar-tugging Crown Prosecutor. Judge McEchern reverts back to a mousy-faced court reporter. Judge McEchern reverts back to a handsome South Asian legal aid lawyer with a black, two-inch ponytail. Judge McEchern is beating the stain out of his judge table with the palm of his right hand. "Stop it stop it stop it," he shouts, trying to outshout the other Judge McEcherns before realizing he is not only the only one shouting but the only Judge McEcherns in the room.

"I'm back," says the elephant-headed witness, grinning, that is if a grin is discernible on an elephant face. "See what I mean?"

"Where are all the other judges?" asks Judge McEchern feebly. "Everyone was a judge just like me." He looks out at the courtroom. "You all changed into me," he says calmly, as one would explain an apparently inexplicable event to a child.

The Crown Prosecutor, tugging at her collar, looks at Judge McEchern and smiles.

The legal aid lawyer, his two-inch ponytail sticking out in defiance, looks at Judge McEchern and smiles.

The court reporter, having decided independently to strike the good judge's comments from the record, looks at Judge McEchern and smiles.

"You did," says Judge McEchern. He looks at the smiling faces. He looks at the witness stand to see an elephant-head grinning at him. Judge McEchern leans back in his judge chair. His hand smarts.

"Court is recessed until ten o'clock tomorrow morning," he says, raising his hand to bang it on the table but thinking better of it and, instead, waving, queen-like, at the court.

DELILAH

I am looking at the contents of the file folder Sandip threw onto the table. I go through each sheet, one by one, although each laser-printed sheet says more or less the same thing.

In Barcelona, in Sao Paulo, in Greenville, in Frobisher Bay, in Ho Chi Minh City, in Adelaide, in Reading, in Munich, in Tijuana, in in in more than a hundred locations worldwide. . . .

Police are stymied by the discovery of a headless elephant carcass and the body-less head of a brown-skinned man.

Another story, just a few lines long, in a hospital in Bhopal, a boy-child is born with the head of an elephant, witnesses say, won't take any food or liquid for three days, then, on the fourth day, he takes his mother's breast, drinks his mother's milk.

I look up at Sandip.

"Why," I ask, "why didn't we hear about these? This, this thing should've hit the wire, all the media, I mean it should be all over the place."

"Yes," says Sandip. "But, you see, I downloaded it from the net."

"So?"

"So I searched for news stories that contained *elephant* and *head* anywhere in their text."

"So?"

"So I defined my search by date," says Sandip calmly. "Starting from the day after tomorrow."

And I look down at the downloaded, crisply-printed sheets and, sure enough, each of them carries a date from the day after tomorrow to several months into the future.

GANAPATI

I look at the Crown Prosecutor with eyes that, I hope, look as human, as compassionate, and as alive as possible. I have spent the entire previous two days convincing the legal aid lawyer that I am, in the flesh, Ganapati. I have exhausted every avenue of logic before the glassy sheen over his eyes dulls just a tad so that, although he might not wholly believe that I am Ganapati, Lord of Wisdom, manifestation of Vighnesvara, Lord of Obstacles, and representative avatar of Ganeshes around the world, he is, at least, not entirely cynical.

The legal aid lawyer, assigned to represent the bodily incarnation of my father, has agreed to introduce me to the Crown Prosecutor in the hopes that we can settle this matter, the desired result being that the Crown stays proceedings and we all go home happy.

The Crown Prosecutor looks at me with exactly the same glassy-eyed sheen it took me two days to only partially soften with the legal aid lawyer.

We have our work cut out for us.

The legal aid lawyer begins by pushing a sheaf of papers across the desk to the Crown Prosecutor. These papers, he tells her, are filled with detailed data including blood work and DNA evidence that shows, beyond a doubt's shadow, that this human body before her, namely, mine, belongs to the discovered head, and that this elephant head, mine again, is the property of the beast's body found in the river valley.

The Crown Prosecutor turns page after page, but she does not look at what is written on them. Instead, she stares at me, glassy-eyed, and with her free hand tugs her collar down so far I can see the top of a scripted tattoo, the first letter either an *L* or an *I* or a *J*, the second letter almost certainly a *Y*, I can see the vee reaching up, and the third the same as the first, there may be more, I can't tell, all encased in what was once a brightly coloured red heart.

After almost three hours – and I am impressed by the short amount of time this takes – the glassy sheen in her eyes has already softened, thanks to very convincing arguments by the legal aid lawyer.

Finally, she sighs deeply and tugs one last vigorous time at her collar. An *L* or a short-hooked *J*, I decide. She looks over at the legal aid lawyer.

"Just as a accused's actual innocence doesn't mean the accused won't be found guilty," says the Crown Prosecutor, "proof that a torso has continued to live doesn't mean we still don't have a homicide, as evidenced by the, uh, dead head."

"That's a travesty of justice, Anna," says the legal aid lawyer, pleased to be able to use the word "travesty" in the same sentence as "justice." "There's been no murder. There's not even been any elephant death. Doncha see? Both beings continue to live, so to speak, right here." He points to me. I smile what I hope will be perceived as both a human and elephant smile.

"Sandip, we can't just make our own rules about homicide."

"Then what should we do? Try, maybe convict, an innocent man?"

The Crown Prosecutor looks at me again. She turns back to the legal aid lawyer.

"See you in court, Sandip."

"I'm going to put the elephant on the stand, Anna."

"It's your head," she says. "And it's McEchern's court."

Hmm. Guess I take the stand after all. I wonder if this Judge McEchern is going to be any easier to convince. Somehow, being lord of wisdom and all, I doubt it.

MR. S

That Crown Prosecutor is lookin' at me like I'm some sorta gargoyle. Sandip warned me that she's gonna try to break me, make me out ta be some sorta sleight-of-hand magician type. So I havta sit here an' answer her questions and somehow this gotta prove that I didn't kill no one. And it's gettin' so I'm not sure anymore myself. Whoever myself is. Yesterday Sandip was all excited, sayin' we had the case wrapped up but I dunno how. When he asked if I remembered the thing with the balls yesterday, I told him yeah, but I couldn't figger out how him throwing some balls at me was gonna prove me innocent. Some balls? That's what he said and his eyebrows crawled up into his scalp. Some, he said. I threw eight at ya, and ya caught them all, he said, each in a different hand. Huh.

Yah, so?

"Dr. Sribhaiman," says the Crown, "perhaps you could enlighten the court? To what end was that 'handy' parlour trick of yours yesterday?" She looks for approval toward the judge, who seems to be very busy writing somethin' down.

"Wasn't no parlour trick," I says.

"All right. Let me put it this way, Dr. Sribhaiman. How many hands am I holding up?" She holds up both her hands. This is silly.

"Two."

"Two. Now, please hold up your hands." So I holds up both my hands and she goes on like this is some sorta miracle. "Ah, I see, now how many hands are you holding up." I look at my left and my right hands, up in the air like I was being robbed or somethin'.

"Two."

"Two," she says emphatically, like this is gonna really interest the court, this little exercise of countin' limbs. "And, Dr. Sribhaiman, how many hands did you have yesterday, that is, when my esteemed colleague over there was throwing balls at you?"

Hmm. That's a hard one. "I don't rightly recall," I admit.

"You don't recall? As in, perhaps you had more than two?"

"Yeah, p'rhaps. I mean, fer sure. Couldn't've caught all them balls with just two hands."

"Ah," she says, and kinda tugs at her collar a bit, "but are we talking about actually having more than two hands or are we now making some sort of reference to what I've earlier mentioned as a 'parlour trick'?"

"Lookit," I says. "You kin call it what ya want. He threw a buncha balls at me an' I caught 'em. No tricks, no extra hands up my sleeves. I just use what I havta."

"I see. So what you're suggesting to the court is, should the occasion arise, you can, shall we say, sprout as many limbs as are necessary?"

I don't get what she's gettin at. "Sure," I say. "That's right."

"Then, Dr. Sribhaiman, I should inform you, this time without you being prepared by your defence counsel I warrant, that the occasion has once more arisen."

Now, this Crown Prosecutor says this whole last little spiel to me while she's gettin' up from her table and kinda scootin' out from behind it and she's like more or less facin' the gallery when she finishes talkin' and reaches into her pocket fer somethin'. Now, I know this sounds crazy, but it's at this exact moment when she starts spinnin' around and pullin' her hand outta her pocket that this little voice tells me to check my shoes, which I do, and sure enough the left one has come undone, don't ask me how I knew. So, even though I figger this is somehow real important I just kinda think well I'll quickly tie up that shoe so's I don't forget when I leave the stand an' maybe trip. So I lean down to do this and just as I do that, kinda dippin' my head below the witness stand, I realize what this Crown Prosecutor is up to.

See, she figgered if Sandip could play with some courtroom theatrics, like, so could she, 'cept instead of jugglin'-balls I kin see that she's got like a whole handful of marbles which she's just throwin' the whole fistful in my direction. Now by this time I'm grippin' onto my laces tryin' to loop them together before anyone really notices, see, and it's all I kin do to just keep my head down so's I don't get swacked with a dozen marbles.

Thing is, I don't figger this Crown Prosecutor's ever bin huntin' and prob'ly never even fired a shotgun, cuz if she had she'd know that shot travels in this V-pattern, spreadin' further outward as it flies. Now, these marbles, gripped in her hand like they was, have the same effect.

'Course, if I'd kept my head up I'd've bin able to catch each and every last one of them marbles, no problem, there's just, like, about twenty of 'em and I've done better, but as it was I figgered I should lay low and tie up that shoelace like the voice told me ta do. Anyways, so a few of them, maybe seven or eight, are pretty close to on target, she's gotta good arm, but, like I say, there's that shotgun V-effect happenin'.

Now in a courtroom, the witness stand is right next to the judge's bench, like right next to it and a bit below. 'Course, it's apparent that this Crown Prosecutor didn't take this into account before tryin' out this gimmick and it also turns out she's gotta bit of a riser in her wrist, so outta the corner of my eye, while I'm tyin up my shoelace and all, I can see about fifteen of these projectiles headin' straight for the ol' Judge's head, an' him acting like nothin' in the world is happenin' mouthin' silently what I think looks like him sayin', "Eighty-eight across."

PARVATI

There are stories within stories. Sometimes people will say there are stories within stories within stories, but those are harder to figure out, because, after all, they could just be making that up.

But, unravelling as this story is, here is one other story. Inside that story where Siva doesn't feel much like hanging around you, where off he goes gallivanting and dancing and where you think enough's enough, gods will be gods, but that's no excuse, and you work up a sweat and make up your own story, a son story, one that comes from you and tells all about you, well, inside that story is this one: after creating said Ganesh, and performing all that suckling and nurturing that, for deity types, takes only the briefest moments, though no telling how many. lifetimes that might be in human terms, you give this Ganesh one task. Yes, this is your story re-told from the start, no differences, no changes in events or names, just details thrown in from source to source. And one of these details, from the source known as *Siva Purana*, says this: you assign Ganesh, still intact by the way, with human head and all, that simple but important task of guarding your bathroom chambers and then, so says this text:

Thus without worry the lovely Lady (that's you) *retired to her* (your) *inner chambers to take her* (your) *bath in the company of her* (your) *lady friends.*

Yes, that's another way your story goes, you and your lady friends and how embarrassing it would be, don't you see, if the Lord Siva were to waltz in on a bath scene such as this? Indeed.

JUDGE McECHERN

Judge McEchern is looking for a six-letter word meaning carnivore when he feels the first one hit. This is rapidly followed by numbers two, three, and four, all of which light into the right side of his face, two into his cheek and two into his chin.

Judge McEchern does not like being a judge anymore.

Just yesterday, in the afternoon, watching television in his den for only about the fourth time since his "accident," Judge McEchern saw a talk show talking about what they called "safe spaces" in the workplace. Now, most of this was dealing with sexual harrassment and how women could build their own networks to protect themselves from, resist, and eventually dismantle systems which provided an unsafe, or what the talk show host called a "poisoned," environment. However, Judge McEchern was not interested in this. He was only interested in how he might be able to change his own particular environment, to create a safe place for himself in his judge's world where, it seemed to him, he was constantly under criticism, under attack, under fire.

To put it briefly, Judge McEchern does not feel safe in his own courtroom.

Numbers five through nine catch him in a nice tight grouping just off his right eyebrow and drifting toward his temple.

In the instinctive moment during which Judge McEchern jerks his head up, his mouth still slightly ajar from mouthing the words "eighty-eight," he is able to make out the tenth and final bead which will eventually strike him making a lazy, loopy path toward his forehead. The middle of his forehead. Right, as they say, between the eyes.

The split second that number ten hits, Judge McEchern makes a mental note to charge the entire courtroom with contempt of court, even the bailiff and the court reporter. However, because he has not written this down, and because the tenth marble is what the kids call a "steelie," Judge McEchern does not charge anyone with contempt of court.

For the briefest of moments, Judge McEchern sees stars. He thought this was just an expression, but this is exactly what happens – Cassiopeia, The Big Dipper, even the Milky Way, trundling across his mental screen in a neat and tidy order.

"Are you all right?" says a voice.

"That one's actually a planet, not a star," says Judge McEchern.

"Sir?"

"Oh, yes, a planet. They look like stars sometimes, silly buggers, but they're not. Just very reflective planets."

"Would you like to lie down?"

"I think that one's Pluto," says Judge McEchern as someone grabs him by the elbows and helps him off his chair. "Although it could be Goofy."

SIDDHI

Delilah Watson is on the witness stand. She is telling the court how she and Simpson came upon the scene of the man's head and the elephant's body. She is telling the court how they proceeded with their investigation, how they interviewed people in the South Asian community, how they began to consider Dr. Sribhaiman a suspect – essentially, how this case came to trial, blemishes of an apparently supernatural nature and all.

But Delilah is doing all this by rote. She has gone over her notes a hundred times and so this is easy. Giving testimony is easy. What is not easy is the way the Crown Prosecutor is asking her questions, or, rather, the way the Crown Prosecutor is looking at Delilah as she asks the witness questions.

"Could you tell us, Detective Watson, what led you to suspect the accused?"

The Crown Prosecutor asks this formally, firmly, but now, instead of really tugging at her collar as she has these entire proceedings and will, undoubtedly, continue to do as these proceedings continue, she is curling her finger around the top of her shirt, loosely, almost casually, thoughtfully.

"Well, that was the fortunate bit," says Delilah, well-rehearsed in her delivery. She wants to make this sound like an off-hand lucky break, which it was, but at the same time not make her and Simpson look completely incompetent. "While we were well on our way toward finding a suspect, we received a phone tip, which confirmed our belief that –"

"Could you tell us about this phone tip?" says the Crown Prosecutor, still playing carelessly with the top of her shirt but her finger trailing down a bit now, down along the stitching of the first buttonhole.

"Yes, it was an anonymous tip. The person, the voice said that we would find what we were looking for at a restaurant, just south of downtown." Delilah is feeling more uncomfortable with the way the Crown Prosecutor is looking at her. As if from the past.

"And did you? Find what you were looking for?" The Crown Prosecutor doesn't really notice that her little finger is tracing the outline of her top buttonhole. What she does notice is that she is looking past the witness, no, not past exactly, but beside. This is strange, thinks the Crown Prosecutor.

"We did. We went to the restaurant, the Ganges on the Thames," a strange name Delilah remembers thinking at the time, but a strange restaurant, too, offering such entries as lamb vindaloo but also odd crossover dishes like curried shepherd's pie and, this item from the lunch menu struck her as quite odd, bangers and daal. The Crown Prosecutor is looking at her oddly. Delilah thinks she must have paused, stuck in memory. And she is and she has, but now not memory of that quirky restaurant, but an old one, almost ancient, girlish, she thinks.

"And what did you find at this Ganges on the Thames?" says the Crown Prosecutor. This witness, this Delilah Watson, is coated with something, thinks the Crown Prosecutor. She has new skin and this new skin is thick.

For a moment, a brief moment, Delilah loses her professional competency on the stand. She is bewildered. She does not remember what they found in the restaurant. She does not even remember why she is in this courtroom. She can only remember what it was like before she ever started this case, before she ever decided to join the force, back when she was in her first year at college, determined as only young folks can be, that she would one day run her own small animal clinic and have her own place, a tiny one, maybe in the city, maybe out of town. Delilah looks over at Sandip. He is busy looking down, shuffling through notes. She looks back at the Crown Prosecutor. She swallows.

"The sword. We found the sword. It was, it was in a mailing tube, a large one, maybe seven feet high, so we couldn't miss it. The owner told us it had been left there some time back, that nobody had claimed it. So, we retained it as evidence." Delilah looks at the Crown Prosecutor to see if this is what she wanted to hear.

For a moment, a brief moment, the Crown Prosecutor loses her professional competency. She is bewildered. She does not register what the witness has said about finding the sword in the restaurant. She does not even register that she is in this courtroom. She can only remember what it was like before she ever started this case, before she ever decided to become a lawyer, back when she was in her second year at college, determined as only young folks can be, that she would make these days last forever. The sound of flowing water, she thinks. The Crown Prosecutor looks up at Judge McEchern. He is busy looking down, writing something and scratching the bumps on his face. She looks back at the witness. She swallows.

"And this sword," says the Crown Prosecutor after what feels like far more than an effective pause, "is this the same sword marked as Exhibit A?" Normally, the Crown Prosecutor would not be so dependent on words. Normally, she would stroll over to the exhibit table and pick up the sword, turn it over in her hands, walk over to the witness box and make sure the witness was sure that this was, indeed, the weapon she had found. But nothing here was normal. For one thing, there was no jury present for her to impress with physical details such as these; for another, that ridiculous excuse for a judge wasn't paying the slightest bit of attention, no doubt trying to find a six-letter word for moron; and for still another, this witness, this cleanly-dressed police detective witness was floating through the Crown Prosecutor's mind as if she were floating in a giant pool of water.

"Yes," says Delilah.

"Very good," says the Crown Prosecutor.

Delilah and the Crown Prosecutor stare at each other through water and through time.

"Um," says the Crown Prosecutor. White porcelain, beige skin, white foam, brown hair, white fingernails, auburn hair, white light. "And this sword led you to the accused?"

"Um," says Delilah. Water in droplets, water in pools, water in hair, water in navels, water in mouths. "The mailing tube. It had an address on it. And a name. S. Sribhaiman."

So, together, what, fifteen years ago, that long ago, skin to skin as water poured foamily filling the tub and their caresses filling the tub neck to neck as water came down. Annie, she says, as water came down and bounced droplets into hair and onto belly. Lylah, she says, as water slipped by them by bodies, thigh to thigh, as water slipped in. The knock. The interruption. The knock. Once. Twice. Hard. Loud. Knockknock. Annie, you in there, his voice, we should have locked the door we should have placed a sentry, knock-knock, heralding his entrance, Annie, oh Annie. Knock. Knock.

Knock. Knock. Judge McEchern bangs the gavel, twice, hard, on top of his judge table.

"Ladies, can we get on with this please?"

The witness, Detective Watson, Delilah, D, Lylah shoots shivs at the judge.

The Crown Prosecutor, *Miz* Block, Anne Block, Anne, Annie shoots shivs at the judge.

"Am I interrupting something in my courtroom?" asks Judge McEchern snidely.

Witness and Crown Prosecutor glow red. Witness reaches for service revolver which, of course, she is not wearing on this her day in court. Crown Prosecutor flexes fingers wishing next week's marbles were spiked with poison.

"No more questions, Your Honour," says the Crown Prosecutor.

"You may step down, Detective Watson," says Judge McEchern.

Delilah leaves the witness stand, walks up to and beside the Crown's table, shoulder brushing shoulder and the sound of rushing water.

MR. S

Why me? That's what I can't figger out. Okay, like, so I've done some readin' on Shiva. So've lotsa people. What makes me special? An' I don't wanna be special. I just wanna do my reading, do my work and that's that. An' anyway, if I was so special, or if I was s'posed to be, how come I can't remember so much of this. I mean, I remember Parvati, mostly, 'cept I still don't remember most of what we did together for, what was it they said, three days? An' I sure as hell don' remember taking off no elephant head. Or the kid's.

And these arms. What about these arms? I look down, I'm perfectly normal, but then whenever I seem ta need 'em, there they are, an' the weirdest part is that when it happens it seems like it's the most normal thing in the world. What about that?

PARVATI

It will all be over soon. Over without so much as a whimper. Over before a thousand sets of remains begin to litter a thousand different cities, bringing talk of a Hindu conspiracy to the fore. Over and done with and back to as it was before.

Of course, there's all these questions, pestering questions, already being asked. Why me, asks the confusable Mr. S, never once pondering the possibility that, in the lives of gods and goddesses, there never is any reason outside of chance. You, you try to tell him, you because you happened upon it this way.

You, because that's the way it is, the way it was, the way it will be.

That's what you say.

But nobody listens to you.

The stories you tell.

GANESH

Mr. and Mrs. Simpson, Dave and Gillian, are arguing. I have been here exactly two months and two days and I know the exact pattern of their arguing. It begins with a minor point of disagreement, and then either Mr. or Mrs., Dave or Gillian, will say to the other, "you're being unreasonable."

"I love him, too, Dave, but I wanted grandchildren."

"Not everyone has grandchildren, Gill. Besides, maybe Nance will have kids once she meets the right fella."

"Oh, my, Dave, you don't suppose Nance hasn't got married because she's, y'know, because she's also, like Gregor?"

"No, I don't, Gill. Now, you're being unreasonable."

See, didn't I say? Now the fight begins in earnest. Soon, quite soon, Gillian, Mrs. Simpson, will begin to cry and Dave, Mr. Simpson, will enact what their marriage counsellor has termed "shutting down" but what Dave, Mr. Simpson, insists on calling "sticking to my principles."

"I am *not* being unreasonable. You *always* say that, but I'm *not*. I just think this might be, you know, one of those things young men go through."

"Gill, he's almost forty. I don't think this is a phase."

"I know," says Gillian, Mrs. Simpson, tears starting to sprout at her ducts and bulge their way out onto her cheeks. "It's just that we never knew and maybe we could have done something."

"Now, now," says Mr. Simpson, Dave, "it's all right. That Sandip seems to be an awful nice guy. And besides," he adds helpfully, "if he was a girl, think of the problems the kids would have, being all mixed up and all."

Mrs. Simpson, Gillian, stops her crying for the moment it takes to admonish Mr. Simpson, Dave, for his voiced racial insensitivity. "That's not nice, Dave," she says politely, "not nice at all. We're all the same in the Lord's eyes, Dave," she says, and resumes crying. "That's it. I can't win," says Dave, Mr. Simpson, throwing up his arms in frustration, an often-practiced gesture, and storming downstairs to his workshop.

He will go into his workshop, slam the door, then open it to see if Mrs. Simpson's, Gillian's, sobs have turned to wails, then shout up the stairs something about this just not working out, and then slam the door again.

I hear the workshop door slam. One, two, three. It opens. Mrs. Simpson, Gillian, has progressed up to the emotional, but not volume, level of a full wail when she hears Dave, Mr. Simpson, yell, "This always happens. I can't take this, I really can't. What do you expect, what am I doing wrong," and the door slams again.

See.

Fighting by the numbers.

GANESH

I am sitting in the dark, waiting for Babiji to come in from the kitchen and light some jasmine or sandalwood incense. She still comes and talks to me and sits beside me, but her face is more drawn these days. She, Babiji, is more sullen, more serious.

She comes into the room now, carrying a packet of matches, a tiny sliver of mehti, and a little creamer she has obviously pilfered from the seniors' club. She sits beside me on the old lavender cushion she reserves for just this purpose. And sighs. She puts the piece of mehti in front of me, lets it sit there for a moment or two in offering as she looks across at me, the picks it up and pops it in her mouth. *Things have changed, behta,* she says, the mehti melting on top of her tongue. She pulls back the foil top from the creamer, just half way, and tentatively holds it up to my trunk. It smells off. Not badly off, but off nonetheless. Off as much as all the milk or cream she has offered me over the past few days. I sniff at it a bit, out of politeness, mostly, but I don't feel like taking a sip. Sorry, Babiji. *Ucha, have it your way,* she says, peels the lid right off and tosses it into her mouth to follow the mehti. She smacks her lips and opens the cover of the matches. She positions a piece of sandalwood incense in the holder near my feet, flicks back the cover from the matchbook, pulls out a cardboard sliver and strikes it alight. She lets the match take hold of the tip of the incense stick, all the while rummaging with her other hand in the folds of her sari. She pulls out her package of Ganesh bidis, takes one out with her lips, and lifts what's remaining of the match to her mouth. *Waste not, want not,* she says, blowing out the match from the corner of her mouth. *I eat your methi, drink your cream, light your incense, smoke my bidi.* She puffs out a stream of smoke over my head. *You have had your fill, ji?*

Sorry, Babiji. I suppose I have.

GANESH

"But Papa, *why* won't he drink anymore?"

"I don't know, behta, that's just the way it goes," says Ravi Gupta. Every day he thinks about that talk show; every night he has dreams where Ganesh comes alive, valiantly slaying scores of Ganas, left and right, striking them down with his staff. Ravi Gupta dreams he has become Kumara, leading those same Ganas to their deaths, conferring with Siva, back when lines did not exist between the heavens and the earth, back in times of Svetakalpa. Ravi Gupta dreams that as Kumara he howls and whines and shouts and sneers and growls and gnashes his teeth, all these threats from different faces, at the disobedient Ganesh, but that Parvati's servant knows no end to his duty. Ravi Gupta dreams that Ganesh starts boofing those brave Ganas over the head with a thick staff, biff boff bam, until they run screaming for cover. Ravi Gupta dreams that even the lords Vishnu and Indra come by for this spectacle and that he, Kumara, six-faced and all, is helpless to stop the noble Ganesh, so helpless in fact that he watches from twelve eyes as the son of Parvati swings freely, lopping off one two three four five heads of Kumara, such that they fling across the heavens and into the universe, become orbiting planets around distant suns. And when Ravi Gupta dreams that he, Kumara, loses his sixth and final head to the warrior Ganesh, well, that's when Ravi Gupta always wakes up.

Ravi Gupta has shared these dreams with me, although, being Ganesh and all, I know them for I have been in them. But he is good to share them with me. And I am sad that he is sad when he tells his youngest daughter, "I don't know why Ganeshji has stopped taking milk. That's just the way it goes."

I am sorry, Ravi Gupta. You have been good to me. What can I say? I don't need any more milk.

GANESH

When Josh Conrad was discharged from the hospital, he tossed me into his gym bag and took me home. I sat in the bottom of his gym bag for three days. It was only when Josh Conrad realized he had run out of clean underwear, and that while the underwear in his gym bag wasn't exactly clean it would have to do until he had a chance to do laundry, that he rediscovered me and set me, where else, but on the top of his TV. As a reminder of better times, he said to himself.

Josh Conrad has a new girlfriend. I can tell by the way he talks with her that she is new and that D'lylah, the woman who gave me to him, was his old girlfriend and that she did not bring him good luck.

He tells this to Priscilla Lane vehemently and frequently. She nods sympathetically when he talks about D'lylah, but I know that Priscilla is secretly trying to get hold of D'lylah, not to talk about Josh, but to get what Priscilla calls the "inside story" to something called the Indian Godfather case. Priscilla does not tell Josh this, apparently because Josh, almost fully recovered although he walks with a tiny limp, and even though he can talk he almost never opens his mouth wide enough for me to see his teeth except for that one time when he yawned and hurt himself and I saw that all his back teeth had silver fillings, is also trying to get this same "inside story."

From where I sit on the television I can see Josh and Priscilla making love on Josh's king-sized bed every second night, whether they both want to or not. It is sort of a ritual, and being interested in rituals, I pay close attention, at least for the first few weeks, but after that I lose interest because the pattern is extremely repetitive and entirely predictable. What is not predictable, and therefore interests me, is the huge, engraved wooden headboard to Josh's bed, which rather reminds me of the friezes at Khujarao except these are done in bas relief and not particularly well done at that, depicting unnaturally shaped men and women engaged in various stages of copulation, attached to the bed by two loose bolts which loosen a bit more with each act of Josh's and Priscilla's own copulation, indeed with each and every very repetitive thrust of each of these acts. I watch with particular interest now, however, because I am certain that one good solid jerk is bound to pop both these bolts off simultaneously, resulting in what I imagine will be quite an obstacle to future lovemaking endeavours.

"You're wonderful," says Priscilla without a hint of authenticity, although such a lacking hint is lost on Josh.

"Am I?" he says, continuing with the same old repetitive motions.

"Yeah, baby, you sure are," she says, rolling her eyes, a rolling which only I can see because Josh is quite intent on performing the task at hand.

"Yeah," says Josh, "you too."

Priscilla has left her beeper in the kitchen. She is expecting a return call, so when the beeper does go off, and it does so quite loudly, Priscilla is ready. With remarkable agility, in the millisecond between the first and second beep, Priscilla manages to extricate herself from under Josh's limbs and appendages and performs a half-twist which lands her, already running, feet on the ground, facing the kitchen.

Josh, excited at the prospect that Priscilla's sudden movements indicate that she is approaching what he always wishes would happen far sooner, that which he calls "her moment," decides impulsively to proceed without caution and finish with what he might call a flurry, but from here looks definitely like one good solid jerk. However, Priscilla's agile manoeuvre which takes her from the bed to the kitchen also has the disorienting effect of flipping Josh from a face-down position to a face-up position, landing him on his back with considerable force upon the bed.

Bolts pop.

Josh opens his eyes, which have been closed for the last two-and-a-half minutes, and perhaps acknowledging that he has lost one lover to a beeping pager, spontaneously opens his arms to embrace another, a hundred-and-twelve pounds of swinging singles carved in bas relief into solid oak.

From the kitchen, naked Priscilla is already speed-dialing the phone number that appears on her pager, the number she has tried several times in the past week and whose owner has finally, thankfully, returned her call. She believes the creaking noise from the bedroom is Josh finishing off, although it seems a rather loud and crescendoing noise, even for Josh, and even more unusual is the piercing scream, abruptly muted in exactly the same fashion as happens when you try to stop someone from screaming by clapping your hand over their mouth, a sound which occurs and is muted at the precise moment the voice at the other end of the line says, "Hello?"

"Oh, hello, Detective Watson?"

"Uh, yes? What was that noise?"

"Priscilla Lane, *Action News*. I dunno. I think something fell."

DELILAH

"You did *what* with her?"

"Simpson, it was a long time ago."

"Officer Watson, I am appalled."

"Simpson. . . ."

"Now, now, D. We're partners. Partners tell each other everything."

"Look, Simpson."

"Why, D. You know of course what this means. This means you're, you're —"

"Simpson!"

"Don't worry. I won't tell the guys. Many of them."

"Look, asshole, that was a long time ago."

"Uh-huh. But you know what they say. Elephants never forget."

SIDDHI

"I didn't recognize you."

"I didn't recognize you."

"I mean, I remembered you. I just mean, you look so different now."

"Me too. I mean, you too."

"What was his name, Annie?"

"I forget."

"Yeah. Me too."

Annie and Lylah laugh. They are remembering his face, how he knocked, how he walked in, the look on his face.

"He was my boyfriend, Lylah. And I forget his name."

Their smiles turn back to laughter, full laughter, growing laughter, his face, their laughter, their uncontrollable laughter. In the midst of this unsubsiding laughter, the cop says to the lawyer: "Hey, Annie, when this is done. . . ."

But she doesn't finish. And they laugh and laugh and laugh.

VIGHNESVARA

I am alive again. Almost. I am almost alive again. No, no, I don't mean literally, or even figuratively, only legally. Legally speaking, if this all works out, and I can't see any real obstacles in the way, I will be legally alive and an undead murder victim. Peachy.

All we have to do is convince one tired old judge that I, or rather, manifestations of myself thereof, did indeed lose my head, neither literally or figuratively, mind you, more or less mythologically, or historically if you place any faith in the greatest of aeons, Svetakalpa, but lose my head I did to my father's wrath in my mother's defence, happens to the best of us, except my father, having de-headed his son, did, in partial obeisance to my mother, grant you, but I harbour a sense or perhaps desire that he did some of this of his own accord and regret, re-head his son, that being me, by similarly deheading a passing elephant, who, said elephant, it should be known, did willingly give of her own head, that Siva's son, a god and a fierce one at that, might live again, and so it came to pass that Ganesh, the elephant-headed one, lord of obstacles known as Vighnesvara, of propitious and auspicious beginnings, hence the god of writing and books, and, insomuch as his, that is to say, my, beginnings were so written, the lord of desire known as Siddhi and also, lest we forget in our lack of wisdom, the Buddhi, Ganapati, lord of wisdom, could live again, not that there was any doubt of that in the first place.

Of course, there's that minor matter of rescheduling events so that Siva himself is re-established as a modern-day Shiva, through the useful and more or less willing participatory model presented to us by our multi-armed and shy but chivalrous Mr. S, the inimitable Sam Sribhaiman, who reconsorted with, my face turns red at such unbridled parental passion, dear mother of us all, but most of all, me, Parvati. And, yes, all of this unleashed by the consequential birth of an elephant-headed boy in an inner-city hospital in Bhopal, home of many million and unfortunate relocation site of Union Carbide; subsequent milk-drinking Ganesh statues around this not entirely global village of ours; revisitations of love, Parvati style, a women-only bathing quarter that is so shamelessly invaded by Sadasiva, now remodeled by upstanding models of the law enforcement and justice system; replicated and multiplied through sordid cities very soon or not at all.

Yup. Should be a snap.

GANESH

I am curled up, nestled comfortably, on Sandip's chest. He is making his closing arguments to the court, and about time, I should say.

He is very eloquent.

"I am not going to tell you, Your Honour, that Sam Sribhaiman is a man who, upon taking temporary leave of his senses, went out and found a still-unreported-as-missing elephant and lopped off his head."

"You're not?" asks Judge McEchern, looking down at the checklist he has painstakingly compiled over the last two days, then carefully crossing out the very first item under *Defence Options* which reads: *he will put forth the suggestion that his client might have done the deed but was not in complete control of his faculties despite the pyschiatric evaluation which found him normal, if a bit forgetful, thus raising the spectre of a temporary loss of sanity without having to enter a plea of guilty.*

"Uh, no, I'm not," replies Sandip, a bit irritated that Judge McEchern seems intent on dialoguing through what should be his, Sandip's, closing monologue. "And I'm not," he continues, "about to suggest that Sam Sribhaiman, through a bizarre series of coincidences that began with a Hindu sage bestowing upon him a relic supposedly that of Lord Shiva's and ending with him being charged with the murder of a man whose identity is still undiscovered, is actually not Sam Sribhaiman, or at least wasn't Sam Sribhaiman at the time of the man and beast killings, but rather an incarnation of the cosmic being referred to as Shiva."

"Oh," says Judge McEchern, poring over his checklist. "That was another *not*, was it not?"

"Yes, a not," says Sandip, waiting patiently as Judge McEchern squints over his list and finally finds the point that says: *he will try to cast reasonable doubt on the identity of the killer by suggesting there was some sort of divine intervention,* and neatly draws a line through it.

"Go on," says Judge McEchern encouragingly, wondering how many more of the Defence Options items the legal aid lawyer will let him cross out before he makes his final decision.

"And I'm not going to suggest that a murder never did take place, inasmuch as a head was indeed discovered but never did the Crown introduce such evidence that would substantiate the perceived or actual death of a person that such a discovery, of a head I mean, would normally denote."

"Ah," says Judge McEchern, crossing off *he will say there's no dead body to prove a murder happened and ask for the charge to be dropped and maybe the Crown might want to lay a new charge of improper disposal of human or animal remains.*

"I merely and humbly submit, Your Honour, that the Crown has not proved beyond a reasonable doubt, or even close to a reasonable doubt I might add, that my client had either motive or opportunity, nor has the Crown proved conclusively that my client was indeed even at the scene of the crime." Sandip looks over at the Crown Prosecutor, who looks at him and nods affably, as if she hasn't heard a word he has said, which, of course, she hasn't, because although she is looking straight at Sandip she has actually constructed an entirely different, and to her far more satisfying, mental image that involves no legal aid lawyer, no aging judge, and no courtly adorned walls, but does involve a lot of water.

"That's it?" asks Judge McEchern, a hint of disappointment in his voice. He still has several items on his checklist that he was sure the legal aid lawyer would address.

"That's it," says Sandip, sitting down swiftly enough that I perform a little bounce on his chest before settling in again.

"But what about the elephant's testimony?"

There is that same fart-hanging silence in the courtroom again.

Judge McEchern squints aggressively at the court, most specifically at the legal aid lawyer. "Aren't you going to mention the elephant's testimony?"

I squirm a bit on Sandip's chest. This ought to be interesting.

"Begging Your Worship's pardon," says Sandip as respectfully as he can while stifling a guffaw, "but did Your Worship say, 'elephant's testimony'?"

"You heard me," grunts Judge McEchern. "What about it? Isn't that going to be part of the defence's closing argument?"

"Ah," says Sandip, wracking his brain for some way out of this, "yes, the elephant's testimony. Well, yes. No, the defence has determined that, while highly, uh, intriguing and somewhat beguiling, the, um, elephant's testimony is not entirely pertinent to the defence's arguments."

"Not pertinent," squalls Judge McEchern. "Why, it's the single most important testimony you've got! I mean, without putting that elephant on the stand, your client would have ended up rotting his life away at Kingston, and you're telling me you're not even going to give that testimony a mention? This is outrageous!"

"Uh, yes. Perhaps the court would grant a brief recess while the defence can, well, assess this situation," says the legal aid lawyer.

Judge McEchern is tired and frustrated and wishes this whole thing would be over. Having made up his mind that he would convict, he is not sure why he is now trying to make the defence's case, except that such a grotesquely misshapen closing argument offends even his sense of justice, jaded as that might be.

He should not grant a recess. The defence doesn't deserve that. And, on top of that, he should charge the legal aid lawyer with contempt, that would teach him to be halfway prepared when he walked into this courtroom.

But, instead, Judge McEchern picks up his gavel and bangs it twice, hard, on his judge table. "Court will recess for fifteen minutes," says Judge McEchern, "so the defence can get its shit together."

VIGHNESVARA

I was afraid this might happen. I think psychologists call this selective, collective amnesia, or some such thing. For deities it's a different matter. It's about stories and narratives and writing things down. If we don't write things down, people forget. And here I am, lord of obstacles, scribe of Vyasa, caught without my pen once again and my trunk down, tusk embarrassingly uninked.

I'm afraid my work is cut out for me.

Fifteen minutes.

Hardly enough time for a tall glass of milk, let alone pulling together a very complicated defence case in this curious murder.

Oh, well, nobody ever said this was going to be easy. Obstacles happen. Time to get to work.

JUDGE McECHERN

"All rise."

Everybody rises.

Judge McEchern walks in, robed in black, sighs as he negotiates the three steps up to his judge table, sets himself down, squints out at the courtroom.

At a very packed courtroom.

At a packed to the rafters right up to where the spider web was but no longer is having been cleaned away despite the fact that Judge McEchern failed to write this down and therefore never told anybody about up there in the top right hand corner of the rear of the courtroom.

Judge McEchern squints and regrets. He regrets he granted this recess instead of somberly finding the accused guilty, putting off sentencing until next week sometime, and going home to a few brandies and Thursday evening television.

In his courtroom are: a man in a neck brace, his face bandaged up so fully that he is unrecognizable; the accused, sitting passively with his hands clasped in front of him, occasionally scratching the top of his head with another hand, the arm of which appears to spring from somewhere indistinct along his body; a bejeweled and beautiful woman whom Judge McEchern has never seen before in his courtroom, but who looks like she belongs and who sits smugly glancing adoringly at the accused, the Crown Prosecutor, a police detective, and several of the elephant-headed people in the gallery; the police detective known as Delilah Watson, who sits in the first row behind and just to the left of the Crown table, leaning forward on the rail with both her hands and staring adoringly at the Crown Prosecutor; the Crown Prosecutor, one Anne Block, who, smiling as though she knew she were being watched, tugs at her collar quite fervently so that the tattooed letters spelling out "Lylah" are singularly visible upon a now-very bright red heart pierced by an arrow just below her right shoulder blade; the police detective known as Gregor Simpson, mirroring his partner's pose but just behind and to the right of the defence table; the legal aid lawyer who, for once, is not shuffling papers nervously but sits back relaxed and even, at the very moment Judge McEchern squints out toward him, turns and blows a full-lipped kiss at the police detective who currently gazes upon him lovingly; an older woman, the one who testified in a language no one understood and no one translated, dressed in a light green sari and, in flagrant disregard of the Court of Queen's Bench regulations prohibiting such, smoking on what looks like a single tightly-rolled leaf of tobacco; another woman sitting next to her, dressed in a grey pantsuit and also flagrantly ignoring courthouse rules by chatting away amiably on a very expensive-looking paper-thin cellular phone; a middle-aged fellow dressed in a suit sitting beside two young girls Judge McEchern presumes to be his daughters by the way he tries to shush them; an elderly couple who, as Judge McEchern squints in their direction, are arguing about the possibility or impossibility of ever having grandchildren and how that does or doesn't matter and what really matters is the happiness of their son; and, of course, legions of elephant heads attached to legions of human bodies, some living, breathing, snorting, and talking, and others carved in soapstone and rosewood and oak and granite or molded in brass and plastic and pewter and glass or formed on silk and cotton and sequined collage, multitudinous, heterogeneous, practical, and fantastical, unending.

All here in his courtroom.

"Well?" asks Judge McEchern. "Are we ready to close?"

"Well," answers the legal aid lawyer. "We are."

Judge McEchern looks down at the notes on his table, the circles and arrows he has drawn to familiarize himself with the various intricacies and incongruities of this case, the notes which sit on top of several weeks' worth of *Times'* crossword puzzles, all immaculately completed. Judge McEchern looks at the paper on his desk. Then up at his courtroom. Then down at the paper on his desk. Then up again at his courtroom. He sighs. Without looking down again, Judge McEchern gathers up all the paper on his desk, pulls it into the centre, begins scrunching it together so the paper mass takes on the form of a rotund ball, perhaps a bit elephant-like, which Judge McEchern pushes and presses and squeezes together until it is one indistinguishable mass, which Judge McEchern then lifts up, holds above his head and tosses, one-handed, way off to the left side of the courtroom where a tiny wastebasket sits, open-mouthed, ready to receive the sphere of judge-paper which circles and twirls spinningly before landing properly and necessarily right in the middle of the basket.

"Two points," says Judge McEchern. "Let us proceed."

"Yes," says the legal aid lawyer, "as to the matter of the elephant, well —" he pauses and looks back at the packed gallery. "Well, as you can see, the supposedly dead elephant and decapitated man —"

"We're here," say a hundred Ganeshes, hardly in unison but with enough force to make their words recognizable. "We're not dead."

"I killed him," says the accused suddenly, "but I put him back together again."

"In a manner of speaking," says the bejeweled and beautiful woman without moving her lips or opening her mouth, and the accused responds by reaching back with four hands the six rows to her seat and caressing her face and shoulders, all the while clasping his hands in front of him and scratching his head.

"And besides," says the woman on the cell-phone, pausing from her conversation to add her bit, "Dr. Sribhaiman is too good a man to commit such a crime."

"This is true," adds the woman smoking a bidi, "my Ganeshji has told me this himself by the way he has stopped taking milk, he is so sick that his very own father might be convicted wrongly," all this in Marathi which, for a brief moment in time, everyone in the court understands.

"Absolutely," concurs the man with the neck brace looking straight ahead at the judge, "this professor is innocent. The real guilty parties are still at large, roaming in bloodthirsty bands through the streets of this fair city."

"Aare, such a saala," says the man in the suit, obviously offended that his daughters have to listen to such sensational lies.

"You're too kind," says the man with the neck brace, swivelling his entire body now so he can see the gentleman who has so generously addressed him, but, not being used to swivelling so swiftly, loses his balance and falls off his chair, his face making full frontal contact with the shiny Ganesh beside him, obviously carved out of obsidian with angular and quite sharp features.

"It is true," says Simpson, leaping to his feet in a moment of passion, "that as the arresting officer I should side with the Crown, but I do have to say that I believe we have charged the wrong man. And I say this not just because I'm in love with the legal aid lawyer. There, I've said it."

"Absolutely," says Delilah, not to be outdone and also jumping to her feet. "Dr. Sribhaiman is innocent beyond question as my partner has stated," and she sits down again amidst the encroaching noise of a tumultuous waterfall.

"There is indeed reasonable doubt, no doubt about that," says a disembodied voice that sounds like it should be coming from a very wise elephant head, "in both human and godly terms."

"No objection here," says another disembodied voice that sounds like it should be coming from the lord of obstacles. "Let's go have some milk."

Finally, there is silence in the courtroom.

"Um," says the legal aid lawyer. "The defence rests, Your Honour."

"Good," says Judge McEchern. "You must be tired." One of the elephant-heads near the back of the courtroom winks at him. Judge McEchern winks back.

"Will the accused please rise," says Judge McEchern to Mr. S.

This Mr. S does.

"Thank you," says Judge McEchern. "But perhaps I should have been more specific. I meant rise to your feet, not rise four feet into the air. That's all right, an honest misunderstanding. That's better."

Judge McEchern pauses and squints out into the gallery. One by one, without any hesitation whatsoever, people and elephants are vanishing. Good, thinks Judge McEchern, that means the parking lot won't be such a zoo when I leave.

"Dr. Sribhaiman. As you might suspect, the court finds you not guilty on all counts. However, I suggest you keep your sword in a safe place. I won't be so light on you if you reappear in my courtroom."

Judge McEchern looks up at his rapidly disappearing audience.

"That goes for the rest of you, too," he admonishes.

The remaining few break into spontaneous applause, cheers, and trumpeting.

Judge McEchern nods an acknowledgement.

"Let's celebrate," a few voices shout.

Why not, thinks Judge McEchern.

Judge McEchern is about to descend the three steps off his judge table, but he is delayed. In front of his bench appears an elephant, a huge one, remarkably decorated and remarkably headless.

"Get on, get on," say many voices, some from visible bodies, others most certainly disembodied. "Get on, you won't regret it."

Judge McEchern shrugs. Why not, he thinks. Why not.

In one sweeping motion, robes arcing gracefully, Judge McEchern arabesques over the bench and onto the elephant's back.

He does not think how he will get off as the elephant slowly trundles down the aisle, out the courtroom, and onto a steamy path along a slow-moving river.

Once up on an elephant, thinks Judge McEchern, once up on an elephant, there's no getting off.

ABOUT THE AUTHOR

Ashok Mathur is completing his Ph.D. in English at the University of Calgary. An editorial board member of *absinthe*, he was a co-founder of disOrientation chapbooks and is an active member of the Writers Union of Canada. He has curated exhibitions of book art in Banff and Vancouver. His book of poetry, *Loveruage: a dance in three parts*, was published in 1993.

Ashok lives in Calgary.

ALSO AVAILABLE FROM ARSENAL PULP PRESS

NON-FICTION

BAD JOBS
CARELLIN BROOKS, ED.
A raucous collection of stories and comics that depict, in gory true-life detail, bad jobs – from beet canning factory worker to Chinese food delivery boy, and everything in between.
$18.95 ($16.95 U.S.)

THE IMAGINARY INDIAN
DANIEL FRANCIS
A fascinating and revealing history of the "Indian" image in Canadian culture. *"Francis has done an amazing job of tracing the perceptions that the dominant culture has had of aboriginal people."* – Books in Canada
$17.95 ($15.95 U.S.)

NATIONAL DREAMS
DANIEL FRANCIS
The stories behind the icons of Canadian history, from the RCMP to the CPR, and how they inform our perceptions of the country. *"A brilliant examination of our national myths."* – Toronto Star
$19.95

O-BON IN CHIMUNESU
CATHERINE LANG
Poignant narratives about the Japanese-Canadian community in Chemainus, B.C. *Winner of the Hubert Evans Non-Fiction Prize.*
$18.95

RESISTANCE AND RENEWAL
CELIA HAIG-BROWN
Newly reprinted: the groundbreaking study of the Kamloops Indian Residential School and its shattering impact on former students. *Winner of the Roderick Haig-Brown Prize.*
$13.95 ($12.95 U.S.)

STONEY CREEK WOMAN: 10TH ANNIVERSARY EDITION
BRIDGET MORAN
The bestselling, award-winning story of Carrier Elder Mary John. *"A valuable and moving biography."* – Books in Canada
$13.95 ($11.95 U.S.)

THE YELLOW PEAR

GU XIONG

In moving words and images, artist Gu Xiong explores issues of identity and culture as an emigré from China. *"Rich in insight that allows us to see the world in a fresh light."* – Vancouver Sun

$12.95

FICTION & POETRY

AMERICAN WHISKEY BAR

MICHAEL TURNER

A remarkable and controversial novel by the author of *Hard Core Logo*: a faux memoir about the "un-making" of a film. *"Brilliant . . . a dazzling, dizzying, multilayered blend of fact and fiction."* – The Globe & Mail

$15.95

AND A BODY TO REMEMBER WITH

CARMEN RODRÍGUEZ

Place and language figure in this luminous story collection based on the author's experience as a Chilean expatriate. *"These stories live and breathe with raw, sensuous energy."* – Vancouver Sun

$15.95 ($12.95 U.S.)

ARCHIVE FOR OUR TIMES

DEAN J. IRVINE, ED.

A publishing landmark: a collection of poetry by the late Dorothy Livesay, one of Canada's greatest woman poets, never before published or collected.

$19.95

THE GHOST OF UNDERSTANDING

JEAN SMITH

A novel by the lead singer of Mecca Normal: at once an intensely personal diary and a rowdy call-to-arms. *"Jean Smith is like a terrorist who demands you read all her diaries."* – Quill & Quire

$14.95

HOT & BOTHERED

KAREN X. TULCHINSKY, ED.

An international collection of short short stories on lesbian desire, including work by Dorothy Allison, Persimmon Blackbridge, Judith Katz, Joan Nestle, Gerry Gomez Pearlberg, and Sarah Schulman.

$16.95 ($14.95 U.S.)

QUICKIES
JAMES C. JOHNSTONE, ED.
An international collection of short short stories on gay male desire,
including work by Perry Brass, Justin Chin, Dennis Denisoff, Michael
Thomas Ford, Michael Lassell, Lawrence Schimel, and Paul Yee.
$16.95 ($14.95 U.S.)

STORIES TO HIDE FROM YOUR MOTHER
TESS FRAGOULIS
Intense, visceral short stories about outsiders – social outlaws
redeemed by their fixations and temptations. *"Gorgeous, stirring and
intelligent."* – Montreal Review of Books
$14.95

Ask for these and other Arsenal Pulp Press titles
at better bookstores. Or get them directly from the press
(please add shipping charges: $3.00 for first book, $1.50 per
book thereafter; Canadian residents add 7% GST):

ARSENAL PULP PRESS
103-1014 Homer Street
Vancouver, B.C.
Canada V6B 2W9

Or call toll-free in North America:
1-888-600-PULP (Visa or Mastercard only).

Write or call for our free catalogue.

Also, check out our website:
www.arsenalpulp.com